THE BOOK OF GOMER

Clent Roye Wyatt

A Midsummer's Lent Book

a novella

CONTENT WARNING

This book includes scenes of a sexually explicit nature, animal slaughter, domestic abuse, infant death, suicide, war, and attempted rape.

It is intended for a mature audience. Reader discretion is advised.

Edited by Em Ramser

Book Design and Layout by Alex Stock

Cover Art by Anna Draussen

ISBN 979-8-9929379-0-9 (paperback)

ISBN 979-8-9929379-1-6 (eBook)

Midsummer's Lent Books

midsummers-lent.com

THE BOOK OF GOMER

A LOVE STORY OF THE SACRED MARRIAGE

To She, From He: I was wrong, I am sorry.

"The beginning of love is the will to let those we love be perfectly themselves, the resolution not to twist them to fit our own image."

– Thomas Merton, *No Man Is an Island*

MAIN CHARACTERS

GOMER – She

HOSEA – He

NOT-LOVED – their daughter

NOT-MINE – their son

THE SHROUDED PRIESTESS – the royal She

THE VEILED KING – the royal He

YEHOSHUA (YESHU) – her uncle

JOSHUA – his friend

HE-HELPS – a local boy

SHRH & YHWH – the deities, She and He

In the Beginning

"God created humanity in God's own image, in the
divine image God created them, male and female
God created them."

– Genesis 1:27

Witness their origination!

Brilliant lights hover over abyssal space. A celestial egg of
suspended matter drifts across while the heavens begin to fall as
tail-trailing comets toward that primordial Earth. Attracted by the
waiting maiden, these questing wayfarers penetrate the globe in
this cosmic dance of the planet's seeding. Life then slowly takes
root, flora and fauna emerging from the depths.

And lo, another miraculous performance of generation is
now heard, the ecstatic sighs of the art of sex, the song of two
entwined. There, in a twilit grove, naked under the trees are they,
He and She. Later, She will grow pregnant and a child will come
into being from her womb.

For now, He and She sleep after their pleasure at the edge
of the wilderness. She remains astride of He, their genitals still
connected. At the first light of morning, wind blowing through the
trees, a voice is discerned. YHWY speaks, "Anthropos."

At that word, He breathes in and opens his eyes.

FIRST COVENANT

Chapter One

Shomron, the watchtower hill, stands strong above the wooded wilderness gathered at its feet and apart from its untamed mountain brethren. Hovels and villages encircle its waist. Upon its shoulders sits the great city of the northern Kingdom of Israel. And the King's shining ivory palace crowns its summit.

The city of Shomron is a city of earthen blocks. Colored tan and pink, the buildings are supported by strong bones of cedar and are decorated with a rainbow mosaic of tilework and gemstones. The closer to the palace, the more intricate and precious is the décor where the richer inhabitants enjoy fabulous fountains for their water and spacious courts filled with rare flower gardens and thrilling menageries. The palace itself is made of milk-white stone and inlaid with an extravagant amount of ivory. Everywhere, the scent of tree resin and the stink of animal dung hang in the warm air.

Outside of the city's defensive wall and halfway down the hill's gentle southern slope is a large dwelling tent nestled under an ancient tree with a twisted and knotted trunk. Stocky and slouched over, the tree is like a wizened grandmother, with its full and sprawling branches stiff as unwashed hair. And there, sitting with her back against the trunk, is She, Gomer. Dark and brooding like the tree, yet unbent, she is the youthful descendant watched over by an arboriform ancestor. Awaiting the day, Gomer watches the rays, preceding the sun, illuminate the mountain peaks and spill into the valleys below.

Her uncle, Yehoshua, known as Yeshu, exits the dwelling. He is a graying, short, and heavy-set man, with a lined face that knows how to frown but is quicker to laugh. He had always been the opposite of his tall, strong, and serious brother. But it was his brother, Gomer's father, that passed away from illness all too soon. And since his death, Yeshu has cared for his niece these last several years. After a brief stretch followed by a deep yawn, he turns to address Gomer. "What has you up from your slumber this early?"

"I had a dream," she replies.

Yeshu snorts and spits, then sits beside her, ready to listen.

She expounds, "I found myself in the midst of Paradise, and there at its center was a great sentinel tree, wrought in the likeness of a chalice, standing watchful and heavy with fruit. At its roots rested a unicorn, coiled around its trunk glided a serpent, and in the branches, displayed, was a peacock. The peacock bent its long neck down as the serpent climbed up, both reaching for the other, and the unicorn turned to look at me." Here she pauses, seemingly reluctant to remember, the black curls of her hair casting a shadow over her face. Haltingly, she relays more, "I could not stand its gaze, so I looked down at my feet, but I could not find them. My legs were lost in coils of roots, and I was unable to move as the unicorn stood, lowered its horn, and…" Her voice trails away along with the gaze of her bright amber eyes as she looks down the hill. She believes she can just perceive the sweet fragrance of the fig trees that grow there in the groves of the Goddess.

Yeshu looks at her and presses for more, "And, what?"

"And? And I do not know. I woke up."

They sit together in silence. As the light grows around them, even the early morning chorus of crickets ceases, and Gomer's dream begins to fade along with the withdrawing shadows.

After a long moment a crow flies overhead. Its hoarse croaking breaks the spell, and Gomer looks over to her uncle. With his eyes closed, she believes he is asleep, until he quickly animates back to the waking world.

"Ah," he exclaims. "Yes, that must be it."

"What?" she asks, surprised by the outburst.

"You feel stuck. Rooted in the work your father left us. Of course, it must be an olive tree, heavy with fruit at the start of the new season." Yeshu thinks some more, then with a smile says, "The unicorn though, that is a sign of good luck, of riches."

"And the serpent and peacock?"

"I do not know. Dinner not sitting well?" he adds with a wink.

Gomer sighs at her uncle.

He laughs, then says, "Come on. The morning is already here, and the olive oil will not sell itself. I'll load the cart for you, and you go get us those riches."

Yeshu stands up and walks back toward the tent while Gomer steals one last glance down the hill then out at the mountains now bright under the disc of the climbing light.

Ω

Later, the sun now peering down from high above the top of Shomron's hill, there amid the people of the city's sunbaked marketplace is He, Hosea, the prophet of YHWY. Tall and serious, he stands above the hustle of the sellers and the buyers. He is a still sundial wand, telling time by his shadow, as he watches Gomer selling her wares from her market stall.

His friend, a handsome, charming, and wealthy man of the city, finds him there and breaks his entrancement. "What are you doing, watching her?"

Coming out of a dream, Hosea looks at his friend, Joshua, who has stood by him since childhood. Even now, though their beliefs and goals have parted from each other, Joshua remains when no other would, as all others Hosea once knew ridicule him for his piety and for letting his father's business fall to the wayside. "I told you friend," Hosea replies. "The Lord has said to me, I am to take her as my wife."

Joshua laughs and says, "You and everyone else. All men want her. And if rumor is true, some have already had her, without the need for—"

"I do not believe in rumors," Hosea says with exasperation. How many times must they have this discussion, he thinks to himself, as he begins to make his way through the crowd. "And it is not lust but duty."

"Alright, not lust," Joshua concedes, walking with his friend. "But only out of duty? What about love?"

"Love is intimate. And I have only known her from afar." Hosea turns to spy her once more. "Love hopefully may come for her and me, after a time."

Joshua eyes his friend, the prophet. He wonders why this man, dedicated to the oneness of the Lord, who has not ever taken a lover, and who preaches against the charms and rituals of the Goddess, would suddenly decide not only to marry, but to pursue Gomer, the very image of the feminine? He warns his religious friend, "I should not have to tell you, if you take her to wife, it might ruin your witness. The King, the priests, they will not listen to your pleas against other gods or against the Goddess."

"My witness is to the Lord. It is he who tells me to do this thing. I have no choice in the matter."

"Yet, she is lovely. You must admit," Joshua declares.

"Of course, I admit. I am not blind." Hosea loves his friend but lately tires at their constant back and forth. He knows their friendship is based on their lives together as children; their fathers having combined efforts in wine production for the city and other settlements in Samaria, of which his friend has taken full control. And he knows Joshua heeds not what he preaches. It is their mutual stubbornness that keeps them together.

"God is truly gracious to you then, to give you such a fine gift," Joshua persists.

Hosea retaliates, "The Lord is gracious in all he does."

Ω

Hosea exits Shomron. He stops just outside the western gate and stands beside the crowded commoners' road to look out at the mountains with their ancient groves, where roots penetrate deep into the stoney soil and branches, laden with fruit for the taking, reach up toward heaven. These are the sacred sites of the wild Goddess and her unruly children.

Walking further, Hosea comes upon two such children, a boy and girl, dancing around a pole, still green from the woods and stood into the earth. "What is this frivolity?" Hosea questions.

"It is an asherim pole," the boy answers.

However, the girl quickly warns him, "Hush! That's the prophet."

Hosea takes the pole from out of the ground and flings it down the hill with a pronouncement, "The wood is only good for burning. If you do not care to burn with it, understand The Lord is God alone."

Ω

After his chastisement of the ungodly children, Hosea resumes his purpose down the hillside and comes upon the dwelling of Gomer. He stops before the threshold and calls in.

The voice of her uncle answers from inside, "Yes? Come in."

He enters the tent and pauses, allowing for his eyes to adjust to the dimness of the interior from the bright day outside. The tent, though now aged and patched, is made from well-crafted skins and fabrics, variously dyed blue, purple, and scarlet. The space itself looms large enough to accommodate a family, the structure being held up by a rectangular frame of strong wooden poles and staked cords. Even standing straight up, as Hosea is, there is room still from his head to the top canvas.

As Hosea stands there, Yeshu, sitting bare-chested in just a coarse underskirt, looks him over while drinking from a skin of fermented goat's milk. Yeshu never cared much for the prophet, especially now with him coming into Yeshu's home adorned with fine breeches and an embroidered linen sash. After a time, Yeshu addresses him, "And what is it the great prophet of The Watchtower would want from me?"

"The Lord wills that I marry your niece."

Yeshu lets the confident statement linger, as he gulps down another swallow of his sour drink. He has become used to men sniffing around for his niece over the last few years. Most of the more prosperous men in the city expect a marriage to come with benefits that further their already considerable social standing, but even they sometimes come seeking after her, considering Gomer enough of a prize in herself. Though the wealthy can still be stingy, as Yeshu has found, and so far he has never seriously considered any offer. Right now, however, he is amused by this chaste prophet of YHWY, striding into his tent and making divine declarations.

"I will tell you, what I have told everyone else," Yeshu finally answers. "I need her here, and if I did not, I would sell her to the ivory palace," he lies, thinking himself sly. "As it stands, I may have inherited her father's meager oil business, but she conducts it."

"The Lord—" Hosea begins but is cut off.

"What can The Lord give me that none of the other suitors have offered? Cattle? Tell me, where do I have to graze them? Gold? Once it is spent, I will be starving and sober soon after. What I have is not much, but it may last a while yet."

"I will give you holdings," Hosea offers.

Incredulous, Yeshu responds, "Carve me off a piece of your family land, where I can then quietly waste away, is that it?"

"No," Hosea continues. "All my holdings. Not just the land, but the home in the city, the cattle, and the vineyard."

Yeshu chokes on his fermented milk. Taken aback by such an extreme offer, and now visibly intrigued, he asks, "And what of you?"

Hosea presses, "We will live here and work your meager oil business in your stead." Then remembering the one truly precious object to him, he adds, "All I reserve for myself from my father's belongings is an ivory horn."

Yeshu considers all of this, overlooking the strange comment of some sentimental keepsake, as Hosea searches him with his eyes.

Before speaking, Yeshu sighs. "Ever since I saw you preaching in the city against the Goddess, against her sacred trees and her rites, saying, 'The Lord is God alone and will reprimand his children of Samaria and Shomron', I knew you were crazy. But this, all for her?" He shifts on his seat and his eyes sharpen. He wonders if he dares do this to Gomer. But he already knows. As if to make sure, he questions Hosea, "You are serious, are you not?"

Hosea, with confidence, asks, "What say you?"

Ω

That evening, Gomer approaches her home and finds her uncle there, waiting, almost lost in the sprawling shadows sent out by that ancient tree she has known her whole life. He walks up to her, carrying a bundle of personal belongings.

"There she is," he says.

She looks at him, dressed in his best robe and wearing his pack, then asks, "Are you going on a journey, Uncle?"

"More than that. I am leaving, moving into the city."

She stops, surprised by this sudden decision, and now wary of his eyes that refuse to meet her own. "How? Why?"

"There is much to explain about this new arrangement," Yeshu begins. He then takes a deep breath and says, "But first let me introduce you to your betrothed."

Staggered, Gomer's head seems to swim as she shouts over this perceived deluge, "My what?"

Hosea exits the tent to find a perplexed and angry Gomer glowering at her uncle like a bird of prey unsure of its quarry.

"I assume you know our resident prophet," Yeshu says, relieved to avert her attention to him.

Gomer turns to look at this man she only casually knew of, and had always thought of as rather boring, and now responds to this imposition with even more puzzlement. "You? You are to be my husband? The one who preaches against the Goddess?"

"Yes. I am," Hosea states.

"No. I will not."

"The Lord wills it so," the prophet insists.

"I will it so," her uncle interjects.

Gomer's confusion suddenly falls away from her like a dam letting out its torrent, as she now pivots her force back onto her uncle. "What do you get out of this?"

"All he has, all his father ever had," Yeshu admits.

"Save my father's horn," Hosea reminds him.

Irritated, Yeshu notes, "Yes, save some ivory horn."

Gomer takes time to breathe, as she looks for a way out of this trap sprung by these two men. "Why me?" she asks Hosea. "We have never once spoken—"

"As is proper for unfamiliar men and women," Hosea interrupts.

"Nonsense," she gives a curt reprisal. "Everyone speaks to everyone in the city these days. Again, why? What would a man of the Divorced Lord want with a wife?"

Hosea hates that mocking title, accusing YHWY of being once married and now separated. "He is not divorced. The Lord was always only ever the One. There is no other god or goddess."

"How very male of you," she remarks. "Both of you," she continues, looking from the prophet to her uncle. "When is this marriage meant to take place?"

Yeshu answers, "No need for delay. I am moving even now."

"I will give you three days," Hosea declares.

Gomer, finding a reprieve, says, "Well then, we are not yet married, so I will retire from the day into my own home, where I know you will not follow."

"Good evening then," Hosea concedes. "I will make preparations and return on the third day."

She enters the tent in a rush for her brief and only sanctuary, leaving the two men in the waning light.

Yeshu looks toward the prophet and, before turning away and up the hill, comments, "Good luck."

Hosea waits and looks up to the walled city, and out at the sun falling behind the mountains. He thinks to himself, he will not need Yeshu's luck.

Ω

Late in the night, Gomer exits her home dressed in traveling attire, a linen skirt and rough-hewn wool mantle, and carrying a pack slung across her shoulder. Pulling a shawl over her hair, she ties it back, then pours a libation onto the roots of her ancient tree, before muttering a prayer. Afterwards, she leaves down the hillside, into the wooded valleys below.

Staying just inside the line of trees, she follows a path around the foot of the Watchtower Hill. She thinks of her father, who would often take her on walks through the wilds when she was a girl. Gomer had grown to love the woods: the dense cedar forest, of course the olive orchards, and the sacred groves of sycamore fig. As she goes, she catches the ripe honey-sweet scent of nearby figs and realizes she must be close to one such sacred site. She walks through a clearing under the light of the moon, when the silhouette of a man slides out from under the darkness.

The stranger calls out to her, "Priestess of the Goddess, Queen of Heaven and Mother to All. I have come to the sacred grove to taste her sacred fruit."

Somehow, hearing that ancient ritual call puts her at ease, like hearing the voice of a loved one, and she surprises herself when she replies, "And what is her name?"

"SHRH," the man speaks in answer. He then moves closer before stopping with sudden recognition in his eyes, exclaiming with disbelief that she is the one he seeks.

Gomer examines the man in his expensive robe and silk sash, with his beard groomed and straight hair clipped so perfectly just above the shoulders she almost mistook it for a wig. With a strong build and visage, he could be the best man at any village game of strength, though with his smooth voice and the grace of his movements, she knows he must be accustomed to visiting the royal court. "Do I know you?" she questions him.

"I live and conduct business in the city, though we have never formally met."

He does seem familiar to Gomer, like one of the many she interacts with at the market. Although she thinks this one is more handsome than most. "And your name?" she asks of him.

"Joshua," he replies. "But are you truly her?"

"The Priestess? No."

He now appears to her to be truly disappointed, lamenting, "Oh, and I thought I was fortunate tonight." Then, he raises his thick eyebrows in curiosity and points out, "But you knew the words."

"Yes, I am familiar," she explains. "I know of it from my mother. Well, from my father's stories of her." Her eyes are downcast as she thinks of the mother she never knew.

"Ah. I never met her." Joshua had heard stories of Gomer's mother, believing her to be a devotee to the Goddess, but he had been young when she passed.

"Well, many men knew her, until she met my father." Gomer had never been ashamed of her mother's promiscuity. Her father hadn't been, so why should she. "They fell in love, and then he was the only one for her. She was very beautiful, so he told me."

Joshua, realizing he has inadvertently brought about a difficult subject, changes the conversation back to the nature of their meeting. "If you are not the Priestess, then what are you doing out here alone at such an hour?"

"Leaving."

"What from?"

"My betrothed."

Joshua laughs then looks at Gomer, who is confused by his mirthful outburst. "Certainly not the prophet?" he asks.

"The same. Why?"

"I know him. He is my friend," he answers. Then as an aside, he states, "He truly did it."

Annoyed, Gomer's eyes flare and she retaliates, saying, "No, he didn't. He may have won over my uncle, but I refuse to be sold like cattle."

"A woman of the new age then?" Joshua inquires, picking some nearby figs and handing one to Gomer.

"New? Has the patriarchy always been?" She lets the fruit drop to the ground.

"As far as I know," he muses aloud, while chewing.

"Not good enough for me. Besides the Goddess is ancient, from before the prophets and their talk of One God. One male god." Striding away, Gomer resumes her journey, then notices the prophet's friend still walking beside her. "You said you were his friend. It seems odd to me then, finding you out here as well."

Joshua shrugs. "We were friends at a young age when our fathers worked together, before he became the man we all know now. And I do not throw away friendships lightly."

A strange bird calls from somewhere in the trees, a melancholy cry like an ancient spirit again newly born and bound to the material world. Both Joshua and Gomer then notice, walking toward them, a shrouded figure, as if the dark under the trees can shape itself and move about freely.

"Your priestess approaches, friend."

"Yes," Joshua agrees. "You better go."

Gomer asks, "You will not tell the prophet, will you?"

"No. But if you change your mind…" he pauses. His eyes are thoughtful, holding compassion for Gomer. He likes her and doesn't want to see her in a cold marriage, but then he wonders what if she could change his friend for the better? "Well, if anyone can show him the good in feminine charm, then surely it is you."

Gomer leaves, silent as the shadows around her, out onto the open path toward the mountains while the Priestess begins an ancient rite of worship.

Ω

After travelling through the night, at dawn she comes to the top of a ridge where the woods begin to fall away, and her view opens. Here she affords herself a moment to look back to the hill of Shomron, the ivory palace at its top glinting with the first rays of the sun.

While Gomer watches the sunrise, another strange avian call heralds the supernal light once again brought forth into the world. Then she turns from that light, and upon the next step of her exodus, a cobra, hidden among the grounded shadows, strikes her heel. In retaliation, she stamps at her attacker and then flees. But as the serpent gives chase, she stumbles and falls among the remaining twilight amidst the stones and roots.

Hoping to crush its head, her hands scrape along the ground, searching for a rock, but before the snake can strike again, a brilliant peacock, all on fire with color, runs into the onslaught. Bringing the sun's light into the darkness, the feathered angel turns the slithering devil from its prey. And

Gomer loses consciousness as the bird of paradise tears into the serpent with godlike fury.

Ω

With some effort, groggy and unsure of where she is or how she came to be there, Gomer awakens beside a warm fire, in a room made of wilderness. The roof and back wall of this alcove are formed from an outcrop of rock with the three other walls closed in by the forest. In the filtered light from an already overcast morning, Gomer sees the snake that struck her, nailed and raised up on a pole. She looks at the fire, as it nurses a kettle, then notices a shrouded woman sitting quiet and still, the Priestess from the night before. Her face is a shadow under her hood, yet her eyes give back the light of the fire. Gomer asks, "Who are you?"

The Priestess replies, "A friend of your mother's."

Gomer remembers her nightly flight, and the serpent… "I was bitten—"

"You will be alright. I have pulled out the venom, but you must rest."

"No. I have to keep going." She realizes she does not even know how much time has passed. Standing, she finds herself unsure on her feet, as her body sways, and sick to her stomach. She retches and falls back down.

"You are too weak for any journey," the Priestess claims. "Rest for now. Then you may travel your true path."

"My true path?" Gomer wonders at the words, confused.

"Yes. One that is hard, one that stands and does not run. One that transforms."

Her voice seems to have a magic and drowsy quality, and Gomer, against her wishes, drifts back into a slumber of uneasy dreams.

Ω

In a forested paradise at twilight, She glides through the trees and, coming into a clearing where the last pale glow of the sun clings to the world, She finds a unicorn standing there in the meadow. Mesmerized, She carefully approaches, as the wonderous beast lowers its head, allowing her to stroke its mane. And then with great fascination, She moves her hand to touch its mystical horn.

But a cry is let loose from somewhere in the wilderness and, as a red moon rises, the startled unicorn backs away, then charges at her, stabbing her through the abdomen. She looks down and, instead of blood, finds leaves growing from her wound as She begins to turn to wood, her toes rooting down into the ground and her fingers and hair spreading out in branches.

Her wooden womb splits open, gushing black sap out onto the ground.

Ω

Gomer rouses again in a sweat, suddenly sitting up and looking around her, still in the wild home of the Priestess. She waits, listening to the trickle of a stream somewhere close at hand and breathing in the ubiquitous aroma of pine. Allowing her mind to calm, she then stands, focused and awkward like a newborn deer. Allowing herself a brief walk, she moves past the trees to a rocky ledge where she sees the first glow of the imminent light of morning.

The Priestess finds her there, saying, "Your fever has broken. We can risk travel tonight." She takes Gomer by the hand and leads her to breakfast. It is a simple offering of bread, olive oil, and figs with watered down wine. To Gomer, after her ordeal, it is a feast as she recognizes how hungry she has become. Thankful, she bites into the fig, letting its sweetness envelop her mouth, then devours all that is given on her plate.

Ω

That night, Gomer walks the wilderness paths under the light of the moon, the shadow that is the cloaked Priestess as her guide.

"Where were you trying to go?" the Priestess asks.

"Away. To one of the outer tribes, maybe. Or south to Judah."

Almost imperceptible, the Priestess shakes her head. "Men are everywhere. You will not change things by running away."

"I will not change anything by playing along either." Gomer's body tenses as she says this, her sinews hardening like iron.

"No," the Priestess agrees. "One cannot change another, but perhaps one could change the self."

They stop. The Priestess takes a large wooden cup from under her robes and hands it to Gomer. It is carved in the likeness of a great tree, black as sin but polished to a heavenly shimmer as it reflects the night sky.

"What is this?" Gomer asks of the Priestess.

"A wedding gift," she answers.

Then Gomer becomes aware of where they have come with the Watchtower City's hill looming above them. "No," she says, handing back the cup.

The Priestess takes it but remains holding it out in offering as she gazes deep into Gomer's face. "There is nothing but sorrow in the outer tribes now," she warns her. "The King soon returns with news, and a plan to keep a great menace at bay. There is no exodus for you, you must turn and fight for what is yours."

"And what is mine?" Gomer appeals for an answer. She is a woman, and nothing has ever truly belonged to her, she knows, as the hot tears of anger just begin to cling around her eyes.

"The Goddess," the Priestess replies with an insistent calm. "The Queen of Heaven has been dethroned, but things were not always thus. It is time we remembered." She presses the cup back toward Gomer. "Take it, it was made from a great tree of SHRH, that once stood upon the watchtower hill, before it was cut and burned."

Gomer pleads with the Priestess. "I do not want this," she says, speaking about much more than the carven chalice.

The eyes of the Priestess, piercing bright from the void under her hood, are steady, but not without empathy. "But this already is yours. Take the cup, it belonged to your mother."

Ω

At sunrise, Hosea is outside Gomer's home, walking the grounds looking for her. He goes back to the front of the dwelling and calls out her name.

She moves toward him from behind, and he turns, surprised, seeing her there standing in traveling clothes and holding a dark wooden cup.

"Oh, here you are," he remarks.

"Here I am," she admits to herself, defeated. "Where else would I be; it is our wedding day."

Chapter Two

With the morning past, on this somber day of her wedding, Gomer is now adorned in simple white robes under a large and delicately embroidered summer-green shawl. The shawl, fitting loosely over her head and falling about her shoulders and down to her knees, has bells sewn into the fringe. The thick, black curls of her long hair also are tied up with a net of tiny jingling bells that sound as she sits, feet unshod, atop a donkey. Her uncle leads the beast of burden up the hill and around the city wall, while she silently stares ahead with her bright eyes of golden amber.

Attempting to break the silence, Yeshu decides to put up a defense. "We both knew this day would eventually come. You could not remain a maiden indefinitely."

They walk further on the path from their home on the southern slope, taking the way by the eastern wall. This way is tradition for a bride living outside the fortifications of the Watchtower City. It bypasses the commoners' crowded western gate, taking them instead straight to the royal north entrance. However, it is slow, due to it being rough and only wide enough for two mounted riders beside each other. On one side stands the wall, dwarfing any that walk under its shadow and constructed of interlocking masonry with outer and inner barriers all filled in by rock and dirt. The other side is a precarious and sudden drop, high above the trees of the forest below.

Only a small, even narrower walkway joins the eastern path and the wilderness; it is cut back and forth into the cliff, and it is known as the way of the dead. Gomer thinks it appropriate that the way of marriage goes past that road of such hopeless finality.

"I understand how you feel," Yeshu drones on. "You think that this was all too sudden and that I sold you for a place in the city. But think of the future. When I die, I have no family of my own, so the property goes back to your husband." Then with enthusiasm, thinking he has it all worked out, he adds, "Meaning it goes to you. And to whatever children you may have. I did not just do this for me, I did it for you."

Without a reply from his niece, Yeshu sighs, trudging onward. Then turning a corner, they come in sight of the gentle northern slope that is the main thoroughfare of the King's Road. Yeshu grows exasperated, impatient for her forgiveness, as they near the great city gate. "Are you going to remain silent forever?"

Gomer thinks of her answer but keeps it to herself. Why should she have a voice now? Her uncle did not need it when he decided who she should marry.

With the day at its zenith, they arrive at the gate. Gomer stares at the two heavy and ornate wooden doors, one for the moon and another for the sun, both depicted anthropologically as lovers. As far as Gomer remembers, they have always stood open and apart.

There, inside the city, waits Hosea. He is in fine white linen which Gomer recognizes to be the vestments of the priesthood and, over that, a robe of dark gray-blue. Atop his head is a billowing cloud of a turban and Gomer thinks he is like a winter storm.

At her coming, Hosea walks out and ties new sandals of supple leather to her feet, signifying his protection over her.

"From now on, you are my beloved," he solemnly swears. He reaches out to help her down off the donkey.

But Gomer withdraws and then clambers off by herself. On the ground she smooths out her robes, her bells jingling as she moves, while Hosea stands back trying to not look embarrassed.

Then leaving her uncle and his pack animal outside the wall, Gomer now walks with Hosea through the doors and into the City on a Hill. However, as they enter, a horn blows, interrupting their simple ceremony of patriarchal guardianship, and a procession of horses and wains comes up the main road, with a herald calling out, "Make way for the King."

The entourage halts in the city square as the citizens gather to glimpse the spectacle. And there, amid the royal cavalcade, the King's personal wagon waits. Open and airy, it is decorated with ivory and covered over with a veil of thin silk revealing only a royal silhouette.

His herald speaks out again, "The King returns from the outer tribes. There, our kin have been at war, fighting off a barbarous invasion, but our King is victorious. The Prince of Peace is he that with a word quelled the savages. Rejoice this day."

The procession starts again toward the ivory palace, as the city begins to move and speak in a sea of babble once more, until the King's hand is revealed, and everything turns still and silent. Then a commanding whisper, the King's own voice, calls out like a stiff breeze, "You, the beautiful bride. Approach. You and your husband."

At first, Gomer is stunned to be noticed by the King, but her feet still walk forward beside Hosea, as ordered. With a sense of foreboding, she finds she is completely unsure of herself, having never been in the presence of his royal person or even of one from his court. She muses on her bad luck, suddenly pulled here and there by the desires of varied masculine powers. But out of her control, there they now stand, She and He, in silence under the gaze of a veiled King.

"I have not seen a beauty such as you outside my palace," the King claims.

"Thank you, my lord," Gomer manages to respond. "I'm only a humble merchant."

"What is it you sell?"

"Olive oil, my lord," she says, looking toward the ground.

The King's shadow, projected on the silk screen, shifts as the attention of its master moves to Hosea. "And the new husband. Do I know you?"

Hosea brazenly answers, "I have been to your royal court, with the Word of our Lord God."

"Ah. The prophet."

A slight wind moves through the city square and the silks part just enough for the prophet of YHWY and his bride to discern keen eyes and a hard smile. They stand, uncertain, waiting on the whim of this man given divine right over all his people and principality.

Gomer shivers, not knowing if it is from the coolness that now permeates the air, or from being caught in the attention of a sovereign of this world. She thinks it unbearable, a grievous wrong that a simple person should be subjected to the realm of the powerful, and that there should never be such a chance encounter. A sense of peril and desire to be left alone builds in her, and she almost yells out, but then she feels Hosea's hand take hers. Something in her settles, and she looks at her husband, finding a strength in his face she had not seen before, an ability to stand under that barrage of royal will. Regaining her own confidence, the spell passes, almost as if a great force has been broken and repelled.

The King speaks again, as if knowing that his power has been resisted. "Farewell, humble merchant with the beauty of the Goddess. If your husband, the prophet, hears God again, perhaps he may share his word with you, and send you to me in his stead. Your company would be most welcome at my palace."

The King's hand motions, and the royal parade moves on, leaving Gomer alone with this strange husband who does not fear the powerful. She then feels ashamed, that Hosea had such an inner strength where she faltered. But then she resolves to remain strong from here on, as she must now contend with him. He looks at her and smiles, but she only looks away, now preoccupied with what to do about the coming night they will spend together in her home.

Ω

Late that afternoon, after signing formal documents at the royal registrar, Hosea and Gomer eat with her uncle in Hosea's family home. The house itself is spacious enough, though lightly furnished, and the back is built into the southern wall of the city, near its eastern corner. Inside, at a table built low to the ground, the new couple sit on cushions in quiet and reserve while Yeshu, in a jovial spirit, is dedicated to food and drink.

Paying them no heed, he holds a cup up in toast, "To the best marriage deal I've ever known. Now do not let the feasting get in the way of the main course, by all means make your way to the marriage bed when you are ready."

Gomer, embarrassed and disdainful, glares at her uncle in hopes of stifling his mood and mouth, but he does not notice. This far into his cup, Yeshu has forgotten his niece's abiding fury, so she resigns back into her sullen silence. It is at this moment that Hosea's friend enters, and all look up from the table to his arrival.

"Welcome, friend," Hosea calls out, thankful for the break in his awkward wedding feast, that even he, being used to silence and scorn, has found near unbearable.

"Happy day to all. I am sorry I was held up, but I have some news which involves all here," Joshua says. He takes a moment to look over the meager reception before pouring himself a drink and swallowing it whole. "It is true, there has been war on the outer tribes. But it is not mere savages, it is the Assyrians that attack. They have even taken land from the tribes Gad and Reuben".

"The Assyrians?" exclaims Gomer, remembering the Priestess's warning. "They live only to kill and conquer."

Yeshu, roused by this news, turns his attention away from the food and wine, for the first time since he began feasting. He adds, "My niece is right, they are nothing but a war machine. They burn the cities that stand against them and kill with weapons of iron. How do we stand against such as this?"

"By keeping them disinterested in conquering," says their friend. "The King has made a sort of peace, by way of appeasement. We help keep that war machine oiled and its red spear will remain pointed elsewhere. Your business is about to become very busy. The palace is opening its coffers to buy up supplies, and among other things, the Assyrians have a taste for olive oil."

Still standing, Joshua lets the news settle, then Yeshu lets go of a booming laugh. "Alright then," he says, "someone else gets a shaft up their end and we get paid for doing our duty to the King."

Gomer, out of habit of laughing at her uncle's antics, cannot help but smile at his crass summary, then realizing her mistake of seeming mirth, quickly turns the corners of her mouth back down.

Hosea has no reaction at all. Unmoved, he is lost in a foreboding mood from the news.

"Sit down, my friend," Yeshu tells Joshua. "And feast with us. Perhaps together we could set the morose married couple to right cheer."

Joshua sits and toasts to the couple. As they eat, he cannot help but watch Gomer with her eyes downcast at her own wedding table.

Ω

Later that evening, after saying farewell to Joshua, the two other men stand in the main room of the city home. There, Hosea hands his uncle-in-law the necessary tokens of ownership to his property. "It is yours now."

"All in good hands," Yeshu assures him. "And it shall be passed back to you in time. I have no desire to share it, while it's mine, with a nagging wife and squalling children. I am too old for any company other than my own."

Hosea nods along, eager to be on his way, then informs Yeshu, "I will visit the land outside the wall one last time and take only that which I have reserved for myself."

"Of course. Peace be with you."

As Hosea walks to a small back room, Yeshu calls for Gomer. "My niece, just one more moment." Gomer gives her uncle her attention as his demeanor sobers. Now quiet and sincere, he searches her face. "Hosea is odd and too religious for anyone's good, but he has sacrificed much to gain you. Try and find some happiness in this, for your own sake."

"Did he sacrifice to gain me, or as he says, out of duty to God?"

Her uncle laughs quietly and says, "That may be what he believes. But I see the way he looks at you. He tries to hide it, but he wants you as any man wants a woman."

This brings no comfort to Gomer as she wonders how she can trust someone who hides what they want, even from their own self?

Yeshu, still feeling guilty, and knowing now the rift between them will not heal quickly, simply says, "Go now. I'll look after you soon."

Slow and dreamlike, Gomer walks to Hosea, who has been waiting for her. In a daze she wishes to draw out time, to delay their night alone. But now, together they stand in a strange and empty room, only the size of a closet, yet exceedingly tall. Set in a wall of interlocking stone blocks, there is a strong but narrow door. And, as Hosea unbars the door, Gomer realizes they are inside the great wall of the city's outer defense, in a small threshold without the rock and debris that fills in the rest of that space surrounding the city.

Hosea opens the passage and together they exit onto a plot of land with grass to graze, a small vineyard, and a barn and storage house. The ground is all enclosed with a stacked stone fence on three sides and the greater wall as the fourth. As they walk across, Gomer realizes that she has often noticed this land, and in fact passed by it this morning, on her way to the path that hugs the eastern wall.

They enter the storage house, a low wood building musty with dust and moldy straw. The last of the sun shines in through the slats, allowing Gomer's eyes to adjust enough to discern walls of sharp harvesting tools and various harnesses for beasts of burden. And in the middle of the floor lies an old dirt-caked carpet, almost imperceptible in the low light from the rest of the floor. Hosea pulls it back to reveal a grate over a hole just big enough for a man to squeeze through.

"What is this?" she asks.

"A family secret," Hosea says in a low voice, as if someone might be listening. "The storage house was built over an old well. It has been dry as long as I can remember but there is a tunnel, perhaps too small for me now, but as a child I could easily play and move about." He raises the grate and lies down on the floor.

Gomer's curiosity is piqued. "Does the tunnel lead anywhere?"

"All the way down the hill, and into the wilderness." Hosea lowers the upper half of his body into the darkness, and calls back to her with an echoed voice, "Here it is." Then he comes back up with a long hide sheath in his hand. "My father's horn."

"What horn is shaped so strangely?" Gomer wonders about its form, still in its wrappings.

Hosea takes a clay oil lamp and flint from a shelf, lights the wick, and then hands the bundle to Gomer. With care, in the small growing light, she unravels the animal skin and pulls out a straight and pointed horn of ivory, a spiral ridge running around its length. For a moment, Gomer only stares at this miracle of being, fumbling for words. "It, it cannot be. Is it—"

"The horn of a unicorn," he answers.

She is unable to take her eyes away from the magical object, the sacred made material. She fears to do so would break the spell and wrest it away from her hands, out of the circles of the Earth, and back to the realm of spirit. Faintly, she hears Hosea speaking to her, explaining how this came to him.

"Before he died, my father gave it to me, with the last words I ever heard him speak, 'There are yet mysteries of God to be revealed in this world.' I took what he said to heart, that is why I first set out to be a priest. I devoted myself to the scriptures, to the law, and to the Temple. The Lord found me there, searching for him, and he opened my eyes to see the disgrace we do him by setting other idols up beside him. It is he alone that works such wonders as what beast this horn must have belonged to, and it is he who still speaks if we would but listen."

Gomer chances looking away from the unicorn's horn, then glancing back to make sure it is still within her hands, she looks at her husband. "Why would God tell you to marry me?"

"He loves us still; he yearns for us," Hosea explains. "I have devoted my life to him, but by doing that, I know not how he feels. I know not what it is to love another." He pauses, then with the light of the lamp playing over their faces, he says, "I did not know until he showed me you. And I confess, though it has been from afar, I have already come to love you, to desire you to be near to me, to cleave to you."

Searching his face, for the first time she feels his gaze not veiled but full upon her, on her body and into her eyes. It makes her feel naked and flushed, at once embarrassed and excited, as she begins to soften and to return his sudden warmth. Then to her surprise, she blushes as her own gaze falters. "Forgive me, I'm not sure—" she struggles to reply. The mystery of the horn has made her forget herself, she thinks.

"I have fallen in love with you. You have time to do the same with me." He puts out his hand and this time she takes it. "Shall we go home?" he asks her.

She nods and they leave the storage house and exit his family's land through a simple gate in the stone fence. Under a clear night sky, they walk to the tent of their dwelling. There, they enter, awkward and unsure of how to be together in their home. Hosea looks around, as Gomer begins to light lamps throughout, revealing a humble but welcoming abode. As he ponders over the intricate floral patterns of the drapery walls and the clean carpeted floor, his eyes fall onto Gomer's carved chalice, reflecting the lamplights like a dark sky full of stars.

He goes to it and picks it up. "Your cup is strange and beautiful."

"It was my mother's," she says, thinking of how the Priestess has had it all these years.

Understanding the importance of family heirlooms, Hosea sets it back down with gentle hands out of reverence.

Gomer blows out her rushlight and they stand apart for a moment, still as statues, as their shadows dance, cast by the flickering flames. "What do we do now?" she says, pondering out loud.

"What would you do, if I were not here?"

Tension is held across the open room, their eyes unmoving from the other's.

"Bathe and then sleep," she states.

"I suppose that will do well enough. A drink first?" He takes a wineskin and undoes the spout.

Before sitting down with him, Gomer retrieves a rough and unadorned cup, which they share between them in silence.

After drinking the dregs, she stands. "I am going to bathe now." She walks to the back of the tent where a large tub sits by a cistern. There, she pulls a curtain up around four wooden pillars, undresses, and pours water over her body with a pitcher, letting it flow from her head down into the tub where she stands. Hosea sits and watches her shape move, a silhouette on the veil between them.

Ω

After his own bath, Hosea finds the oil lamps extinguished excepting the one he carries, and Gomer on her bedding, with her back turned to him and a fur brought up above her waist despite the warm night air. He hesitates, staring at her shoulders and her hair falling like night in black curls, coursing along with the curve of her body. Sitting down on the pallet of rugs and furs, he longs to feel her. Reaching out to touch her, he pauses, his hand suspended in air.

Gomer remains still, holding her breath, her eyes open in the dark, away from the light where he cannot see.

Hosea pulls back. "Not until you want me, as I want you." Then he turns away, before he changes his mind, and lies down next to her.

The tension falls, and Gomer's body relaxes, though her eyes remain wide and waiting, drinking in the dark. She remains this way, until she can hear him breathing slow and steady. Carefully, she rolls over and sees his eyes are closed. Tired and ready to give herself over to sleep, she is suddenly taken by a wakeful curiosity and spares a moment to look over this man she does not know, yet now shares her home and her bed.

He keeps his hair short, and his wooly beard has a dark, ruddy quality. She's met many handsomer men, though he is not uncomely, with a youthful, almost boyish face that Gomer believes strangely contrasts to his deep, often authoritative voice. While his body is slender, she does find it harder, more used to labor than she had imagined, and looking down, she sees his desire for her showing strong even in his sleep. Then, realizing she is staring, she grabs the last lantern, blows it out, turns back around, and closes her eyes.

Ω

In the morning light diffused through the tent walls, Gomer wakes alone in her bed. She dresses and walks outside to find Hosea pressing olives, with sweat already on his brow. Approaching, while watching his work, she notices spent olives, from past presses he had smashed whole, in a mess on the ground.

Hosea looks up from his labor and pauses to catch his breath, managing a salutation. She responds in kind, and he stands a bit longer waiting for some small praise for the work he has already put in. After no more than an expression of mild interest from her, he goes back to the press as she looks on. Easing the pressure lever, he then pulls off the cover and tosses more of the mashed olives onto the ground.

"How long have you been working?" she asks him.

"Since first light."

"How much oil have you now?"

He bends down and grabs the clay container, from under the spout, just now filled to the top. With a large smile, he answers, "A full jar."

She smiles back and even laughs. Happy to have received such a joyous response to his hard work, he goes back to it with great exuberance.

"You are doing it wrong."

Suddenly crestfallen, Hosea realizes her laugh was at his expense. "How so?" he wonders.

"You do not press whole olives. You will never get enough oil that way. They must be ground before the pressing."

Pitifully, he exclaims, "Oh."

She walks toward him. "Why did you not wait for me to show you?"

"I wanted to surprise you," he says.

"I am surprised."

Embarrassed, he looks around at the waste he has made with his morning. He decides to accept his mistake and move ahead with his plan to acquaint himself with his newfound work, albeit this time learning from his wife instead of assuming and hoping to impress. "Where do we grind the olives?" he asks.

"We do not. Another family down the hill does and then brings the grounds here for pressing." She points to a pulled cart coming up the winding hill way, remarking, "See, here they are coming."

Hosea picks up the basket of olives he had been pressing. "Then what are these meant for?"

"I picked those for eating." She takes one, pops it into her mouth and smiles again as she goes to meet the cart; her husband watching her go.

Later, they work the press together, as she instructs him. The ground olives come in sheets of woven platters as many layers are fitted into the vat at once. Hosea thinks of Gomer like an instructor at temple, gesticulating and lecturing, as she guides him from over his shoulder to press the same vat multiple times, and scolds him when he fails to change jars before one overflows. She works him hard and enjoys it. And at the end of the day, Hosea is impressed with both Gomer's expertise and the amount of product they produced.

Ω

After their work, both tired and worn, they retire for the evening. While Hosea bathes, Gomer tallies their output using a clay tablet and reed stylus.

He speaks to her from the bath, "What do we do tomorrow?"

"We will take the oil we have to market."

"How often is that?"

"Twice a week, maybe more, once production increases. As more people pick, the more will be ground, and the more we will have to press."

He pulls the curtain away and she watches him as he grabs a fur to cover his nakedness. "You run your family's business well," he says.

"Thank you." She goes back to her markings, but having lost her concentration, she sets the tablet and stylus down, then looks back at Hosea. "Your help was welcome today."

"You were a good teacher." Though strict, he thinks with a smile.

After she bathes, Gomer goes to her bed and sits with a fur pulled over her, watching Hosea bent over some writing. "Do you read well?" she asks.

"I do. And I write."

"With ink and parchment?"

"Yes, though I have none with me now." He sets down a pile of scrolls and looks over at Gomer.

She speaks, "My father was going to teach me, before he died."

"You already read and write," Hosea insists.

"I do not."

"I saw you, marking our production on the tablets."

Gomer shakes her head. "That is different."

"Numbers or words, it is all only symbols. Everything is language."

Incredulous, Gomer asks, "What do you mean, everything?"

"Everything," Hosea speaks with enthusiasm. It is now his turn to show his expertise. "'And the Lord spoke, and it was so.' You and I are only words in his great story." Hosea holds up what he has been reading. "The book of Genesis," he explains, then sets the vellum down, and blows out his light.

He lies down next to Gomer, who again lays with her back to him and a fur over her body. In the dark, he speaks to her still, "I can teach you."

The proposal excites her. She turns to him, smiling, and forgetting the fur, she lets it fall away from her body. "Please, do."

They lay for a moment, only a small space between them. Then she turns back around, draping her fur back over herself, a covering of the sacred, glanced for a moment then hidden again from the sight of man.

Ω

Some days later, Gomer is selling at the market, when Hosea walks to their stall. "How are we doing?" he inquires.

"Well enough. Where have you been?"

Evading the question, Hosea responds, "Are you already missing me?"

Gomer smiles at him, as she has begun to relish his advances, and even more so, she delights in her retreats, keeping him in this quest. It is a power over him she did not expect to have. "Not yet. Only curious. Does selling at market bore you?"

"I do not get bored with you near to me. But I had some small business to attend."

Her smile subtly fades, as she remembers who this man is. And she wonders at the difference she sees, almost as if there were two of him, in his warm and endearing relationship to her, and in his cold and unmoving beliefs of a God without love or need of the feminine. "Did you have an urge to preach?" she asks.

"No. I haven't had such a word from the Lord. He has left me be a while."

With this confession, Gomer believes she sees relief in his demeanor. She lets her smile return, and with that light falling upon him, Hosea is inspired to declare, as he has many times since their wedding, his love for her. "Right now, my beloved, only you matter."

They stand there together, as if they are the only two people in the city, until a growing line of customers, now calling out for her, brings Gomer's attention back to her market stall.

Ω

Sitting alone, outside their dwelling place as the sun begins to set, Gomer marks down their profits for the day. The horizon grows to a dark red, and the mountains a deep purple. Everywhere around the hill, the inside of tents and windows belonging to humble shelters light up and the smell of dinners being cooked around the community waft through the air. When Gomer enters her own home, she finds a small meal laid out, and on a low table a stack of blank parchment sits with a new inkwell and quill.

"Are you ready for your first lesson?" she hears Hosea ask.

Gomer looks over to him with delight written across her face. "Where do I begin?"

"We will work on your lettering. Writing the alphabet is the best way to memorization."

They sit down together, and taking the quill into his hand, Hosea dips the point into the ink. "The first letter is Aleph." He writes it down, then hands the quill to her, saying, "Now, your turn."

She draws out an aleph as the ink begins to run. Then, looking upon the deformed and bleeding letter, she frowns.

Hosea assures her, "Writing is an art; you must feel it first to know how the ink flows. Try it again."

Close together, huddled over their writing implements as if by a warm fire, they take turns marking symbols onto empty sheets, laughing at the mistakes they make as the ink works against them with a life of its own.

Ω

Deep in the night, Hosea is asleep, as Gomer lies next to him wide awake. A growing and steady desire has her bothered and animates her from her bed and across the room to where his father's horn sits next to her mother's chalice of SHRH. She takes the ivory unicorn's horn and runs the length of it through her hands, examining it up close as if it were harboring mysteries she might deduce by careful observation. Afterward, she places it back, setting it point down inside the chalice, instead of beside and apart. Then she goes back to bed, her body turned toward Hosea, as her eyes slowly close.

Ω

In the afternoon of the next day, husband and wife work the olive press together. Today feels different to Hosea, as his glances toward Gomer are now met with her own eyes already upon him and accompanied with furtive, knowing smiles. It seems to him as if a shroud has lifted from between them.

"I think that is enough work for today," she announces.

"It is early," he says, surprised.

"Yes. I will be in the tent." She goes in, and he finishes bottling their last press.

Hosea then enters the tent, as Gomer finishes bathing, and he takes his own bath as she oils and perfumes her hair, filling their home with the sweet and earthy scent of frankincense. After drying, Hosea finds Gomer with a fur draped over her shoulders and offering him wine from her own black chalice. He takes and drinks, then she drinks, all the while her eyes not leaving his.

"Will you write with me again?" she asks.

They sit together and write until, losing interest, she looks up into his face. Taking the quill from him, she sets it down, then shrugs her animal skin off, letting it slide away from her to the ground.

He is entranced, fixated on her. First, he reaches out and simply caresses her shoulder and then feels the thickness of her hair as he allows his eyes to take in her body. But he soon finds that it is her own eyes, lamps of golden light, that most holds his attention.

She removes his own skin of fur, and they kiss, as all his thought falls into her, intoxicated by the taste of her mouth. Then pulling back, but not far, she takes his hand and places it between her legs. With her own hand over his, she teaches him how to search her out. And as he caresses her, they breathe together, his other hand holding her hair away from her face, all the while seeking her further still, eyes and body, until he feels her open to him.

"Now?" he is hardly able to ask with one exhalation.

Biting her full and flushed lip, all she can do is shake her head, yes.

And he takes all of her. Pulling her onto him, his hands grasping her bottom, he enters her, and she moans as he gasps then sighs. They embrace and begin to move their flesh together as one. Then, laying her onto her back, they spill the inkwell. And as they fuck each other, letting their passion pour into one another, they leave markings, symbols of their desire written in ink over their bodies.

Ω

That night they cleave together; even in their sleep, they are bound, one to another. And the next market day, they share not-so-secret glances between them, and they laugh together in front of busy customers. They close early, and almost run home, hand in hand, immediately undressing each other after entering the tent of their dwelling.

Afterwards, she bathes with the curtain veil no longer drawn between them. A shadow no more, it is her body revealed in the light, form and content, naked for him to behold.

Ω

A season passes this way, under the sun and under the moon. They work the oil press. They fuck each other. They sell at market. They fuck each other. They practice reading and writing. They fuck each other. She grows pregnant. They fuck each other.

Chapter Three

On a morning many months later, Gomer's uncle, Yehoshua, rides a donkey out the gate from his plot of land, pulling a small wagon. As he winds his way down the hill, closer to his old home, he hears the playful laughter of his niece and her husband as they go about their work. Approaching, he calls out in greeting, and both husband and wife return salutations.

Yeshu loves what has become of them. It makes him feel happy for his niece and vindicated for his decision. Reigning in the donkey, he looks at Gomer's hands on her swollen abdomen. "I see your belly is greater every day."

"Yes, the baby is growing strong," she states with pride showing in her demeanor.

"The mother is strong," Hosea adds, lending a hand to help the older man down. Then glancing up the hill, he asks of Yeshu, "How goes it behind the wall of our watchtower city?" Hosea and Yeshu then begin loading jars of oil onto the wagon while Gomer rests under the shade of her tree. "It goes well enough," Yeshu replies. "The gold of the ivory palace is flowing, but the King demands more and more. Other oil presses have already doubled their production."

"It should not be a problem," Hosea comments. "We can hire an extra hand if we need. However, as our earthly king makes demands, it is now time to see to the demands of our heavenly Lord."

Yeshu makes a sour face at this idea. "You're going to Temple this season?"

Hosea explains, "It is timely to give of our first fruits now as our first child will soon be born."

Yeshu had thought perhaps Gomer had cured this man of his zealotry. "Damn devout prophet. And I was beginning to think you had given up on your insanity. At least you have been too busy with my niece to go preaching."

Hosea laughs at the sudden ire of his uncle-in-law. "The word of our Lord has not changed even if I take time to love my wife."

Yeshu pleads with Hosea, hoping for pragmatism to win him over. "But I need you here. I need you working."

Hosea hands him some coins. "Here. This can pay someone to work the press while we are away."

Yeshu takes the money with a frown.

"And to pay for a lamb, if you would be kind enough to bring us one from your flock."

His face only grows more downcast.

"And rent for your donkey."

Now, Yeshu's face twists and contorts.

Hosea presses the matter, "Of course, you would not want your pregnant niece to go without. And these first fruits belong to you as much as us. The Lord will look kindly unto you."

Yeshu senses there is no persuading his fanatic of a nephew-in-law and instead seeks to inspire some moderation.

"At least, tell me you are not fool enough to go to our estranged southern kin. They have no love for us."

"To Solomon's Temple? Indeed, I am fool enough. But no, for the sake of my wife I will take the shorter journey to Bethel."

Yeshu gives in, contented by Hosea's compromise. He glances toward his niece, then in a low voice says, "Good. These are dangerous times. I have even heard rumors from your friend that the southern King of Judah seeks to make war against us with the Assyrians. It seems we are in a bidding race of who can best appease this foreign army."

Hosea nods in agreement. "As much as I believe the Temple in Jerusalem is the true house of our Lord, we are a people broken in two and at such times must do what we can. I pray we do not break further."

Yeshu sighs. "Offer your prayers then and go offer your sacrifices. Let me make arrangements before I see you off."

Hosea thanks him.

Yeshu looks Hosea over and shakes his head. His niece has changed, softened and brightened, from coming to love this man. And though he believes Hosea does love her in return, he now wonders if that love has changed the prophet at all. "As if you really cared for my approval," Yeshu says in response to Hosea's thanks. "I like you, I really do, despite you. But be careful, the man who believes himself the arbiter of God is the man who believes himself above all others."

"I am a servant only."

"A servant only of the Most High, and none other," Yeshu says, chuckling. "I cannot stop you from going, so I might as well wish you a safe journey." He pulls himself up onto his donkey and calls out to Gomer a goodbye.

She waves from under the darkness of her tree as her uncle rides back up the hill of Shomron.

That night, in the tent of their dwelling, the two lovers lay together on their marriage bed, quiet and at ease. She lightly draws her fingers across his body when she looks up into his countenance. "I am happy here with you. May these days last forever."

Ω

A week later, they leave on the same way Gomer had taken during her failed flight, where the serpent had filled her with venom and the bird of paradise had descended upon the devil, a site of sudden woe as well as unexpected salvation. In the distance lies their Watchtower City on a Hill, all alight and shining, until a wind blows an errant cloud, darkening the ivory palace.

After traveling through the mountain path, Gomer atop a donkey and their sacrificial lamb in tow, the land begins to flatten into a near featureless plain of short brown grass, dotted sparingly with thickets of brush. Small thrushes chitter about as the lonely travelers wander along.

A few days out on the flatland, as the sun sets and bleeds the horizon, their familiar mountains are now only a distant dark line behind them. Gomer brings in the lamb from grazing and sits beside her husband. Hosea has been reading by lamplight next to a small camping tent.

"What are you reading?" she asks.

"An account of Elijah. He ascends the Mountain of God. The same mountain where the Lord had descended to bring revelation to Moses. Mount Horeb, though some call it Sinai." As Hosea speaks, a faraway look grows in his eyes. He realizes he is jealous of those prophets before him, the two, that not only heard the word of the Lord, but rose to such a height as to be in his presence upon the world. Hosea's life has been forfeit for so long, given into the Lord's hands, as he has come to know control is an illusion and all fate belongs to God. For this reason, he does not fear the worldly powers. He only has one fear, and it is the same of his desire. To know the Lord, to be found by him, and enveloped, baptized by that highest power, fills him both with an existential fear and yet great longing. But that was before, he confesses to himself, as now he has found, for the first time in his adult life, that he is confused, split in two.

The Lord is no longer his only desire, and with his love for Gomer and his unborn child, his fears have multiplied and brought his thoughts down to the mundane, thoughts of leaving his holy quest, and living a small life for himself, and for his family. He wonders, why would the Lord put this on him? He was the one who commanded Hosea to take Gomer to wife. Was it only a test he was meant to refuse, to remain faithful? How can a man be split between the sacred and the profane?

Suddenly, his mind comes back to where he is. "Moses and Elijah, they both met the Lord on that mountain."

"Why not again?" Gomer muses.

Hosea is caught off guard by the question. "Why not again, what?" he asks of her.

"Meeting God," she exclaims. "Many people say God is found on the mountaintops, yet I have heard say God is everywhere. In the stories of our own people, God met with others than Moses and Elijah, and met them wherever they were, valley or wilderness. And why now do you prophets say God is no longer found even on the high places but only in his house, a temple built by men?"

Somewhere inside of himself, Hosea is impressed by her insight, but he is exhausted by his own newfound uncertainty and by giving her a passionless and patronizing answer he is in some way trying to reinforce his own challenged beliefs. "It is the way of the law. The law the Lord gave to Moses," he tells her.

"Yet, Elijah found God once more on the mountain. After Moses. After David and Solomon. He did not have to go to the temple." Gomer is exhilarated by her own intuition, relishing a chance to show her husband what she has learned from reading his scriptures and that she is not unwise in these matters, as she remembers her father being open to discussion and instructing her in various beliefs when she was younger.

But, Hosea responds, coldly, "It is the way for the people, as a whole. Only a few may truly be in the presence of the Lord."

Gomer, indignant at his declaration and of the way he callously spurns her thoughts, presses the matter further. "Why? Why not us all? Why not even a woman?"

"We are unclean."

Gomer pulls away from him. "We? You mean the people? But not you? You, Moses, and Elijah are clean?"

Now he responds impatiently to her passion. "I mean we. All are unclean, but—"

"Then if one unclean human is allowed, why not all?" she interrupts.

"I do not claim to know the mind of the Lord."

"Only his word? You claim to know that," she mentions.

"I know what he speaks to me. Nothing more, not even why he speaks to me, why he chooses who he chooses."

He sighs, and she sits back at an impasse with him, as the last of the sun disappears. She wonders again at the seemingly two Hoseas: her husband who is kind, loving, patient, and open to learning from others, and the prophet who defiantly refuses to move when discussing spiritual matters, making every point a hill to die on.

Hosea tries to put the contention to rest. "Come, let us speak to each other as man and wife do, and retire for the night."

This casual abatement, of a matter of importance to her, almost reignites her argument, but then he sets his hand on her belly and in that moment they both jump, reacting to the life growing in her womb.

"Did you feel that?" she asks.

"How could I not? Our child is restless."

"I will probably be kept up tonight."

"Then I will stay up with you."

Pacified, they leave the argument unresolved.

Ω

In the morning, He exits the tent, leaving behind his wife. There, He stands in wonder, looking up at a single great mountain though the land was level the evening before. On either side of the summit are the sun and the moon. He begins to climb. Halfway, in the shaded side of the mountain, hidden from the sun, He finds She, waiting for him.

"Go back. I must do this alone," He calls to her.

"Why not together?"

"No. I am. Alone," He insists.

"But are we not one?" she asks.

"Go back." He resumes his climb, and at the top finds the sun just above the peak, warming the world around him.

There again is She, waiting for him.

"What are you doing here?" He asks of her. "Leave me. I must find God," He declares.

"It is only us here. You and I. We are." She reaches out her hand to him.

He only walks past her, in a panic, looking for something He cannot see. "Lord, where are you? I am here."

"Will you not take my hand? Will we not be one?" She begs. As She speaks, with her hand still held out, the light begins to darken.

He looks up at a dimming sun, high in the sky. "What is this? What is happening?" He cries.

The sun is overtaken and blotted out until a black hole hangs overhead, like an abyss opened above the mountain peak, and a great net of uncanny twilight is cast over the world.

He is fallen over on his knees while She is now weeping and pleading with him, "Please, take my hand. Be with me, before our moment passes."

He looks up with fear in his face and begins to reach out his hand to her, just as a ray of light again lances out from the black disc. She recoils as her hand goes to her belly, and She screams out in agony as a river of blood is let loose from her womb and falls over the mountainside, filling the valleys of the world below.

Ω

"I am sorry," Hosea cries out, waking to the twilight in their small travel tent and grabbing Gomer's hand.

"What? What is it?" she manages to ask, startled away from her slumber.

Confused, Hosea mutters, "I am, we were, I do not know." Then he begins coming to his senses, back to the world of the waking, and away from the shadows of dreaming. "I am sorry, it was a dream."

"It is past now," she consoles him. "It is already past."

But he draws back at her words, momentarily slipping back into his subconscious world, remembering where She had spoken of a passing moment of portent. "What did you say? What is past?"

"Your dream. It is past. Are you okay?" She grabs his hand and holds it tight.

The warmth of her hand in his calms his mind. "Yes. Sorry, I will be fine. I am only shaken."

"Come. I will not sleep anymore, so we might as well break our fast." She lets go and readies herself for the morning before the sun.

Ω

That day they travel in silence. Gomer, atop the donkey, casually takes in the world around her, as the grass has given way to dirt, rock, and scrub. She comforts the sacrificial lamb next to her pregnant belly, running her fingers through its soft, greasy wool and breathing in its sour, sweet scent.

Hosea walks ahead on the path yet is lost somewhere within himself.

After a time, they begin to slope up a low hill and, cresting it, find an altar built of piled stones under a tree. Hosea seems to rouse to wakefulness and goes to investigate the devilry. The stones he finds to be stained with blood and smoke, and inside a hollow of the tree is a carven figurine of a woman with large breasts and a protruding abdomen.

"Why have we stopped?" Gomer asks. "It is only some pagan's altar."

Hosea takes the wooden idol and dashes it in two against the stones, with a passionless duty. He then tears the altar down, rock by rock, before resuming their journey.

Gomer sits for a while, stirring within, then can no longer hold back. "You did not have to do that."

"Please, let us not argue today."

She refuses to leave this alone. "As we go to worship and sacrifice, you would destroy someone else's way to do the same?"

"Yes. Because what they worship is false. The Lord is not in wood."

"It is only an image," she remarks.

"An image of a foreign goddess," he says with only a low sigh, as he keeps leading their route forward.

"Foreign? Some say she has always been with us, that she is the feminine counterpart of the Lord."

"The Lord is only one, no more," he declares.

"If God is one, why a male? Where is the female?"

Hosea believes her thinking faulty, stuck in a material understanding, and tries to end the argument. Ceasing his path, he turns around. "You speak out of ignorance. The Lord is neither male nor female. He is spirit."

Gomer cannot believe how blind Hosea is to his own language. "Like you said, 'He' is spirit. He is certainly masculine then. You prophets and priests speak of husband and father. What of wife? What of mother?"

"It is only symbolic. We are his people, as a wife to her husband or a child to the father."

Gomer shakes her head in desperation to be heard. "But it still has meaning. Words matter; they are matter." She remembers Hosea's lesson on the book of Genesis. "You said so yourself, that words are everything. The world is created from language, words the threads that weave and bond reality together. If God is spoken of as male, then God is male. Does the feminine not share in divinity?"

"His word matters. Not ours," Hosea claims, agitated, resuming his way forward.

"Then say 'She!' The Lord is She!"

He is silent.

She presses, "Our words matter."

Gomer slides off the donkey with the lamb, letting it jump from her, and attempts to catch up to her husband, now recalling another matter of language. "I remember when you first started preaching. It was not against the Goddess then, but against a pagan group worshipping Baal. Did you stop to wonder why they came to Shomron, why they wanted to speak with us Israelites? My father spoke with them. They wanted to know more about the Lord. They worshipped the Lord."

"Not our Lord."

"Yes, they were asking for us to share with them what we knew of the Lord. There are many languages and words for God and The Lord, you did not bother to translate because you were too prideful to think they might love the same Lord as you. What does the title matter, El Elyon or Elohim, or Adonai. What matter if they speak Baal—"

"A foreign word for a foreign god," he interjects.

"—or even YHWY."

He stops and turns around to face her, yelling, "How dare you let that holy name slip from your lips."

"It is only a name," she challenges him. "How dare you judge those who would seek you out as a brother in God. Does anyone belong to God other than you and dead forefathers in dusty pages? You say you want to bring people to the Lord, but all you do is turn them away."

Hosea's face is now red, and his hand raised. "Enough. I have heard enough blasphemy from my wife today to last me my lifetime."

Everything stops, and Gomer's eyes move to that hand poised in the air, then move back cold and pointed, daring, straight into Hosea's face.

His countenance falters, his hand, his eyes, his being falls within, ashamed of his affront, yet still angry at her words.

"Why can we not speak with each other?" she pleads, exasperated.

"There is nothing to say on such matters. The Lord has spoken, he gave the law," he says with a weight behind his words. "There are no new revelations, and no other covenant, only a deeper understanding, an intense fidelity to what is already given us."

"And what of love?" she wonders.

"What of it? All, even love, is subordinate to the law."

Gomer stares through Hosea. She cannot believe his words, that anything would be greater than love. But they go on, Hosea now focused on the way ahead of his feet, trying to take his mind from Gomer. He does not see her, behind him, silently weeping.

Ω

The next day, they arrive in sight of the Temple of Bethel, House of God, and camp near an ancient well where they drink their fill and give water to their animals. Hosea pitches their tent, as an open canopy, and they rest under its shade, looking out over the open land scattered with rock and shrub, and at the village around the walls of Bethel in the distance.

Both are tired, but not from travel. Hosea has increasingly become disturbed by the dream he had and from the arguments he and his wife have engaged in. He feels that the Lord is near, that soon the divine gaze will be full upon him, and while always frightening, before it had always been accompanied by a sense of fulfillment. Now, he only dreads it, and that also frightens him. But, with their destination in sight, his mood lifts and his attention turns to the rift between him and his wife. Before this journey, the two of them had been as one, and that close relationship, he thinks, had been built by such patient work towards a shared trust. Looking at her now, however, she has no more smile for him. "Do you need more water?" he asks her.

She simply responds with a negative, as she quietly plays with the doomed lamb to pass the time, one hand patting it on the head and the other resting on her belly.

Looking toward the walls around that holy place, Hosea remembers the time he stayed in Bethel pursuing his old goal of becoming a High Priest of the Temple, this House of God patterning itself and its class of priests on the one of Solomon in Jerusalem.

"I spent several years here, training for the priesthood," he begins, speaking aloud while still staring ahead. "My father had also trained, as he is descended from those Levites that settled in our northern kingdom, that claim the sonship of Aaron along with those ministers in Judah. But he was captured by invaders, while defending Bethel, only later to be released. He then wandered the Earth, and returned to Samaria, a rich and worldly man. I loved him, but I also loved the scriptures he taught me to read." Hosea looks behind him at Gomer. "I suppose my path has not been so different than his, as we both began here, then left our family's destiny behind, finding our true purpose." He smiles. "I was sitting here when the Lord first spoke to me. Later, I convinced the priests to take down the idols they allowed the people to worship, but it was hard fought, and my preaching left more than a few at odds with me. That is when I turned aside from the priesthood and returned to Shomron as the Lord's prophet of our Watchtower City."

Gomer looks over at her husband. "Did you see the Ark of the Covenant, while training?"

"No. Though I always desired to travel to the Temple in Judah. I have yet to do so, and with the two kingdoms splitting further and further, I believe just as Moses never entered our promised land, the Temple of Solomon will remain my unfulfilled desire. But, as to being in that most holy presence, I gave that up when I left the priesthood. Only the High Priest goes into the Holy of Holies."

"What of those here in Bethel?"

"The High Priest of Bethel is permitted the journey, and to witness its majesty, as they all belong to a brotherhood of secrets. The Ark itself resided here for a time, and the Holy of Holies of Bethel conceals its own mystery."

"Do none ever share what they have seen?"

"None ever do. But I assume that is as it should be, or so I used to think. The priesthood is often contradictory, as they are the keepers of the holy relics, and the mediators between the Lord and his people. But they so often lower themselves to please the whims of their flock and the royal line of kings. That is why the Lord must raise up prophets, choosing those that will not dilute his word. And the priests of secrets often grow contemptuous."

"Why then have we come?"

"The Lord speaks his word to me, but all are held to the law, even I, and we must still make our atonement, even if the keepers of the temple law have become lesser."

Gomer thinks over the journey they have taken, wishing they had never left. Though today he tries to hide it, something has come over her husband. He has been irritable, angry, and despondent. She thinks it must have something to do with the temple, as she watches him staring ahead at his goal with an agitated pensiveness.

Ω

That night, as the lamb wanders, chewing on tufts of grass shot up from cracks in the hard dirt, Hosea remains watchful over the temple. Finding it hard to sleep, he tries to relax by looking up into the dark sky of heaven, filled with stars. As he does, one star, a shining one, lights up the sky in a great burning brilliance, overtaking the heavens, and then falls from its appointed place. Streaking across the empyreal plane, and down to Earth, it strikes the foundations of the House of God.

Hosea jumps to his feet and runs forward, believing Bethel must now be burning from the fiery fallen star, but being blinded in the dark from the great light of its descent, he stumbles and falls. On the ground he looks up, as his eyes clear, to see his lamb standing above him. The innocent beast looks full upon him and speaks, "The Ladder of God falls from Heaven to Earth."

Hosea looks from the lamb to the House of God, only to find it peaceful and quiet, no sign of destruction, no sign of the fallen heavens. He turns back to the lamb, and it just bleats at him like a dumb beast then leaves to find more grass. Hosea slumps down into the dirt and ponders at this sign of God that has transpired.

Ω

Hosea rouses Gomer at first light. "It is time to enter Bethel."

She blinks her eyes at him and sits up. "Have you slept?" she asks him.

He does not respond but instead begins packing for the day.

As they begin walking, Gomer notices they almost imperceptibly travel downwards. Looking out about the landscape, she realizes that Bethel sits at the bottom of a shallow but wide basin, as if the House of God itself was so heavy it pulled the earth around it down.

At the temple wall, an old priest comes to greet them, recognizing Hosea. "Good day. How has the time been since you last visited?"

"The Lord has blessed me many times over," Hosea responds. "Please, meet my wife."

Gomer nods down at the two men of God, from atop her donkey. While the temple priest and her prophet speak, she finds it ironic and amusing how the former seems himself to be a sacrificial lamb with his wooly white hair and wobbly voice. Further studying the older man's fussy demeanor, she notes his guarded eyes and careful words. She then surmises through his pleasantries that he is wary of her husband's presence and seems to want to hurry them along.

Now the priest takes more than a cursory glance at Gomer and exclaims, "Ah, you are pregnant. You have been blessed."

Hosea explains, "Yes, we will sacrifice first fruits for our many blessings. And we plan to wait here to give birth so we may then present the child to the Lord."

"Very good," the priest says, but betrays his unease with a sour, pinched face. Then motioning to the lamb, he asks, "And is this your offering?"

"Yes, and a jar of olive oil," Hosea answers.

"Then let us proceed into the court, of course your wife will wait there with the other women."

They move within the wall following the priest with his bobbing gait into the courtyard. Gomer takes it all in. Along the inner wall wait the women and children, as they watch a priest perform the sacrificial rites of burning offerings at the large altar. Smoke and the smell of charred meat is so heavy in the air it stings the eyes.

In the middle of the court is the sanctuary with its threshold between two giant bronze pillars and its doors overlain with gold. Gomer knows she will never see inside that sanctuary, the Holy Place, but she also knows within is hid another inner sanctuary, the Holy of Holies. She looks at her husband and finds his eyes cold and dark. As he stares ahead, she follows his gaze and there, its limbs looming over the sanctuary, stands a tree with a great Goddess carved into the trunk, majestic in her countenance and dreadful power in her hand.

It is an affront to Hosea that this stands in the temple dedicated to his Lord. "Why is this still here?" he asks.

The priest looks at the prophet, not wanting to revisit these old divisions. "We took your advice to heart, you will notice we removed the sun-image and the golden calf, but the people…" he pauses. "Well, they cried out for their Goddess. It was best to leave her be."

"To appease the people? What of the Lord? Do we no longer care to appease him? Destruction will come from this," he says, now using his authoritative and sonorous prophet's voice. He turns to Gomer and commands, "Be ready to leave." Then he takes the jar of oil and the lamb and strides toward the sanctuary, the old priest shambling behind him.

"What are you doing?" cries the priest.

"This is no longer the House of God. It is the House of Nothing." Entering the sanctuary, Hosea grabs a ritual knife from a small altar at the door. Then opening the clay jar, he lets the oil pour out, anointing the lamb. And he advances toward the veiled threshold of the innermost chamber.

"Do not enter, you are not of the priesthood," the old priest warns.

"And this is not the true Temple of Solomon," Hosea pronounces.

"Please, this place was consecrated by Israel himself."

Hosea pauses, wavering in his purpose, remembering the story of their forebear, Jacob, his dream of a ladder between heaven and earth, and the sanctification of this place. Momentarily he wonders, could such a holy path, a way to God, found before the commandments at Moses's Mountain and before the Holy Ark of that covenant, remain there just behind this hanging cloth?

The priest, believing he now has Hosea's ear, seeks to persuade him further. "Do you know what sits upon the Ark of God? Even in the temple at Jerusalem, there is worship to the Goddess." But his words only give resolve to Hosea.

"Then we all are no longer his people." He cuts the throat of the anointed lamb as it gargles on its own blood, then throws the innocent sacrifice into the northern Holy of Holies, tearing down the separating curtain, revealing nothing, only a strange glossy-black stone half-embedded in the ground.

Gomer waits at the outer wall sitting on her donkey, as priests run toward the entrance of the sanctuary. Then she sees her husband, the prophet, bloodied and coming toward her. He takes the donkey and leads it out, leaving Bethel behind.

Ω

On their journey back to Shomron, they travel in silence. Gomer's concerns for her husband's state of mind increase. "What happened in the sanctuary?" she finally asks.

He remains silent.

"Will you not speak with me?"

"The fear of the Lord is upon me," he abruptly states.

Gomer remembers being caught and singled out by the King on their wedding day. She remembers the unbearable burden she felt, how she wanted only to escape his gaze. And she thinks, if God does single out her husband so, how frightful that must be, more than any earthly ruler.

But Hosea has been so hard and cold since their journey, so angry, and now distant, barely even there in his body. She finds it hard to want to console him and believes he would not accept it even if she could. She considers, if this is what his God makes of a person, who otherwise can be so warm and gentle and full of love, then she wants nothing to do with such a divine power.

It pains her, but at least for now, she chooses to let him be, and indeed his declaration of the fear of God is the only time he speaks to her for the duration. And as their path wears on, he becomes even more dejected, weighed down and muttering to himself.

Ω

Near the end of their return, as evening falls, they move around a mountain cliff. The hill of Shomron comes into view at the last light of the sun, painting it all red, and with the moon full and bright white, hanging over the city.

Hosea hears a commotion on the side of the path and looks to see a white peacock and a great black snake together in a death struggle. The bird of paradise has the serpent's tail in its beak, already beginning to choke it down. The snake reaches around and unhinges its jaws, swallowing a foot of its adversary. Both the bird and the serpent, either one being too large, attempt to consume the other.

Hosea then, turning back to Shomron, is struck down by a vison, filling the sky. "Lord, no," he wails. "The City on a Hill burns."

Shomron seems under siege by an army of great clouds of shadow, brandishing lightning, as the city burns. The army, like a terrible wind, blows at the northern gate which shudders from the force, and the sound of it reverberates down the valley and up the mountainside as thunder.

Above the destruction stands a cosmic woman of apocalypse, the smoke and ash slithering up to her as an offering of incense. Her blue-black skin is clothed in the setting light of the sun. Her eyes shine red, intoxicated with rage, as her tongue lolls from her mouth. And she is crowned by twelve stars. With her legs spread from horizon to horizon she tears open reality, birthing into the world a great moon-pale egg which descends into the nest of flame.

Now prostrate on the ground, Hosea calls out, "The whore mother gives birth. The fruit of our iniquities."

Then the watchtower hill quakes with a great rending sound, like a multitude of trumpets, and an abominable beast with two faces bursts forth from the great gate of the city. In announcement, the fierce Goddess roars around the Earth one word, "Anthropos."

The vision passes as Hosea gawks at Gomer standing over him. With waking life back in his eyes, she begins to question, "What happened? You screamed out nonsense and fell to the ground."

He answers, "I have seen the destruction of Shomron. The Lord will bring swift justice, the spear of the Assyrians, for our sins."

Chapter Four

Some days later, at dawn, Gomer wakes in the tent of their dwelling to find Hosea reading scripture by lamplight. This is all he has done, she thinks, since he was stricken down by his vision. To her, however, it is not divine but madness.

"Have you even slept?" she asks him.

"Some."

"Will you take the oil to market today? We cannot eat scrolls of ink and parchment."

"Yes. I will go." He leaves, later that day, with a meager amount of oil.

Ω

At the olive press is a quiet, young, but hardy boy they have kept at work since her uncle hired him in their absence. Gomer hands the boy a piece of bread while he breaks. "What is your name?" she asks the boy.

"He-helps."

She laughs, like there is some joke the boy does not understand. He seems confused and offended.

"Do not worry," she assures him. "It is a common name, although also noble. You share it with both prophets and kings."

The boy looks sheepish, now assuaged by her words.

All the men in Gomer's life seem to be of one kind, she thinks: Hosea, Yehoshua, Joshua, even the King. They all share this mutual moniker. "It seems my lot to be surrounded by helpers and saviors," Gomer muses.

She returns to her tent where she half-heartedly practices her letters. Then, bored, Gomer begins to bathe herself. As she pours the water over her, the sensation flowing down her skin calms her and Gomer begins to study in her mind her tempestuous marriage. Then, despite herself, she smiles when she remembers their intimacy and Hosea's once persistent passion for her. He was so kind and patient, but now it seems like some spiritual malady that takes hold of him. She resolves to fight for Hosea, even against God, and win his heart back to her.

But then she winces from a pain in her abdomen, and looking down in the tub sees the water has turned a pale red. Putting her hand between her thighs, she pulls it back, stained with blood. She grabs her under-linen, and in haste pulls it over herself as she runs out the tent to He-helps. "Go find my husband at the market, hurry."

The boy looks at Gomer in her wet and sheer garments, embarrassed, then notices the growing spot of red and turns, running up the hill.

Near the city gates he meets Joshua, who recognizes him. "Boy, where are you going in such a hurry?"

"The prophet's wife. She is bleeding," He-helps responds.

Concerned, Joshua joins the boy, and they both run to the market stall, finding it abandoned. He tells He-helps, "Go back to her, do whatever she needs of you. I will find the prophet."

The boy runs back out the city and down the hill and into the tent. "He is not there," he gets out in gasps.

Gomer, now curled into a ball on the ground, looks up with pain and fear on her face. He-helps is frightened by the amount of blood on her.

"Do you know where the grove of the Goddess is?" she asks.

The boy does not answer, only staring.

"Do you know her sacred grove?" she cries.

He manages to shake his head in affirmation.

Gomer lets out a beleaguered breath. "Go there and bring the Priestess here."

The boy's eyes grow wide and he slowly backs away, unsure. "The Priestess? No—" he mumbles.

"Yes. Do it now. Go," she demands.

He-helps tears through the tent, down to the bottom of the hill, up another rocky slope and into a close stand of sycamore fig, where the air is thick with a drowsy sweet scent. The boy stops, as his hands go to his knees, and gasps for breath. Looking around, but without seeing anyone, he yells out at the trees around him. "Help. Please, help. The prophet's wife, she needs you. Are you here?"

A shadow moves from under the trees and into the light, her voice ringing out, "I will go to her. Run before me, tell her I am coming."

Ω

As Gomer bleeds, and the Priestess moves up the hill, Hosea is on the steps to the ivory palace. He has been prophesying, as a crowd gathers around him.

"Woe to the Watchtower City, Woe to the City on a Hill. Destruction is upon us," his voice roils around the courtyard. "The king can no longer appease the Assyrians, as he cannot appease the whore goddess. For both are insatiable. The Lord has loved us as a husband and father, but he can no longer look upon our transgressions. He will give us over to our illicit lovers, he will deliver us to this foreign army and to the Whore of Sheol, and we will be devoured by fire."

The crowd murmurs, a few throw curses, as some voice agreement.

Joshua finds him there, as he is speaking. "Hosea," his long-time confidant shouts above the din of people.

Hosea searches the crowd, narrowing his eyes, and locates his friend. Some primal emotion written across Joshua's face makes Hosea waver in his oratory. Fear, he thinks. Joshua is afraid. Hosea jumps down the steps into the throng and meets him. "What is the matter?"

"It is your wife. She needs you."

"The baby?" Hosea asks. His knees give out momentarily, but the pressing in of the people keep him on his feet.

"I do not know. But you must go to her."

"What's going on with the prophet," someone shouts, as the crowd closes further in.

"Something about his wife," another answers.

A drunkard makes a crude comment about Gomer and laughter erupts.

"No. It's his baby," a woman yells.

Hosea's head starts to sway.

"What kind of prophet can't keep his own child from harm?" he hears someone accuse.

Joshua grabs Hosea's shoulders and steadies him. Hosea's mind then clears with a singular goal and the two men gather their strength, pushing through the now oppressive presence of the masses.

Ω

That evening, the Priestess, arrayed in her dark cloak, approaches Gomer and Hosea's dwelling place. First, she goes to the tree beside the family tent and cuts off a leafy branch, then sticks it into the ground before the entrance as if planting a sapling. She enters the tent, finding He-helps there, offering water to Gomer. With eyes only upon the bloodied and feverish prophet's wife, she points her words toward the young boy, commanding, "leave us."

He-helps leaves the tent like an arrow loosed from a bow, as the Priestess begins to weave word spells and burn incense, filling the room with a sweet and thin white cloud.

Ω

At sunset, Hosea and his friend race down the hill when the boy runs across their path. Joshua stops to try and question him, but He-helps no longer listens, fleeing away.

Hosea, however, now having gained near his home, can hear Gomer screaming along with a low and steady chant, and then silence. He tears through the pillar of smoke at the entrance and sees the Priestess over his bloody wife. "What is this witchcraft?"

The shrouded woman turns holding his infant boy, not squalling but wheezing. "A son is born to you this day," she says.

Hosea takes the boy, warily, seeing the baby is frail and much smaller than he should be. Then with fear and scorn, he tells the Priestess, "Get out. You are not welcome here."

"The Goddess protects the mother and child. Both are weak, they need my help."

"Leave," he demands.

She looks at Gomer, back to Hosea, then turns to leave. "As you wish, but do not fail to administer the medicines I have prepared. They are not yet out of danger." Exiting the tent, she stops to speak with Joshua. "Help him see to his wife. The bleeding has stopped, but she needs rest." Then she glides down the hill, blending in with the growing shadows.

Ω

That night, Hosea sits up by Gomer, who is delirious from fever and loss of blood. He cools her with a wet cloth, as their wheezing baby lies swaddled next to her.

Joshua enters. "Here is the mare's milk for the child, still warm."

"Thank you," Hosea replies.

"I can stay up with you," Joshua offers.

"No. They need rest and prayer. You go sleep and see to us in the morning."

Their friend stands with a look of concern then leaves.

Gomer, weak, begins to speak, "Medicine."

Hosea looks over the poultices and elixirs the Priestess had left, potions and remedies of the Goddess. "Why did you bring her in here?"

"Medicine, please."

He brings the chalky preparation to Gomer's lips, and she drinks it down. Soothed, she falls asleep, and Hosea picks up his son. He feeds the newborn some mare's milk, sucked from a pinhole in a sheep's bladder, but most of it is spit back up.

Then, while taking the Priestess's medicine to administer to his child, a wind comes into the tent and blows out his oil lamp. Hosea feels his way back over to Gomer and sets their infant down. Lighting a rushlight, he goes to the entrance of the tent to tie it closed when he notices the tree branch sticking up in the ground just outside, and a name scratched into the dirt: SHRH.

In a sudden fury, he takes the branch and breaks it and stomps out the name of the Goddess. Then with conviction he gathers up the medicines, her unholy craft, and throws them out into the darkness. "We need prayer," he cries out. And he begins to beseech his Lord.

$$\Omega$$

At the hour of dawn, Hosea is asleep, having fallen over in a heap during prayer. Gomer slowly opens her eyes and searches to find her son beside her, to look on his face.

In that early morning pale light, around the Watchtower Hill, a terrible wail is heard assailing from out the tent of their dwelling, rushing up to the walls of the city of Shomron and down into the valley below.

$$\Omega$$

Late in the day, Gomer lies down, staring at the space near her, where once there was a baby boy for a brief time. Hosea enters and pauses wavering in what to do, distraught and tired. He glances at Gomer but then goes to his scriptures.

"Where were you?" she questions him.

"What do you mean?"

"I sent He-helps to find you. You were not at the market."

"I was doing the work of—"

"You were preaching. You should have been here."

Hosea refuses the blame and stands in defiance. "You are right. I should have been here. To keep that witch from cursing this home."

"Curse? The only curse in this home came upon it with you," she accuses.

Convinced in his faith, he counters, "You desecrated us by bringing the befouled goddess in here."

Gomer laughs at him, as he stares at her, thinking she has gone mad with grief. Finally, she chokes back her outburst to spit at him her welling of contempt. "How blind are you? The Goddess was here before you."

"What are you saying?" Hosea asks, the room darkening around him as if some unseen assailant lies in wait.

"My family worshipped her. My father and mother," Gomer professes. "My carven cup you like so much, it belongs to She, to SHRH."

Hosea feels as if a trap has sprung on him. "You have profaned me," he shouts.

"How? It was the Lord who told you to marry me," she reminds him. "Perhaps he was wrong."

"He is wrong in nothing."

"He did not save our son," she screams like a spirit wallowing in damnation. "You prayed all night, and our son is dead."

"Stop it."

"The Goddess would have saved our baby," Gomer asserts.

"Enough."

"You killed him, when you refused her remedies."

Hosea takes her carven chalice and smashes it down on the ground, over and over, until it splinters into pieces.

Gomer laughs, and then cries, and then laughs through her tears.

"Why did the Lord give me a harlot for a wife," Hosea laments.

Gomer stares at him, her eyes wide, and then whispers in a hiss, "Divorce me."

Hosea is silent through his distress, studying her, this woman he thought he knew. Her amber eyes he once thought like the honeyed light of heaven now seem of hellfire. He manages his answer, "No."

Ω

In the night, Hosea sleeps, but Gomer lies awake. Silent, she rises, letting her covers slip away. Stalking across the open room, she takes Hosea's sacred horn. She holds it, lightly running it through her fingers, and then she takes it between her thighs, sliding it back and forth slowly, rhythmically, until she sighs and then quicker, until she moans.

Hosea wakes. Hearing the commotion of her ecstasy, he shines a light upon her and catches her defiling his father's ivory horn, as she takes it into herself. All at once flushed with sudden adrenaline, anger, and arousal, Hosea nearly jumps off his bedding.

Gomer orgasms, smiling at him right before he strikes her down. From the ground, she looks up at him, standing over her. "Divorce me. Let me go," she demands.

He pleads with her, "I will not. Please, stop this madness."

Gomer sees that, despite his objections to her lewd behavior, Hosea has an erection, and she takes him into her hand to pleasure him.

"Stop," he implores, retreating away from her.

She approaches, on her knees, and grabs him again. "If you ever loved me, please let me go," she begs.

"I told you, no."

As she strokes him faster, she claims, "You called me your beloved. I believed you, I even thought maybe I loved you too."

Hosea's resolve weakens and Gomer finishes, spilling his seed on the ground, a sexual taboo against his Lord.

"There," she declares triumphantly. "Another abomination to the Lord. Now, how else will you let me curse you?"

"You are delirious," he contends, with sorrow and fear welling up from his throat. "Some devil has taken over you in your anguish."

"Divorce me," she wails. And jumping up, she grabs her fur and races out of their dwelling place, into the dark.

Hosea cries out after her, but she is already gone, lost in the night. Unsure of which way she went, and too frightened to look again upon her hate-possessed visage, Hosea falls to the ground, seeking his Lord through prayer.

Ω

Before the twilight hour, their friend is awoken from his slumber at his house in the city. Joshua sits up, listening in the dark, and hears knocking at his door. With speed, he lights a lamp, covers himself with his robe, and opens his home. There he finds Gomer distressed and barely covered by an animal skin.

"What is wrong?" Joshua wonders.

"Nothing is wrong," she answers.

Joshua blinks, still not fully awake. In a dreamy and casual manner, he remarks, "Oh, that's good." But then he still is confounded to find her at his door in the dark of night. "I am sorry, is there something I can do for you?"

"Yes. There is," she replies. Gomer walks past him and into his home. She turns to him, her shape visible in the lamplight, her fur haphazardly draped from her shoulders. "You are fortunate tonight."

SECOND COVENANT

Some years pass, and one morning, there is a visitor at Yehoshua's entrance. Yeshu shuffles from his kitchen and sits onto a bench in his main room with a grunt. His previously graying head has now lost all color, and his robust weight has been lost as well, leaving someone not hale and lean but sunken in and wasting away.

"Enter," he calls out to whomever.

Joshua comes in, time having taken nothing from him except perhaps his blithe spirit, and sits opposite.

"It has been a while," Yeshu recalls.

Joshua nods and inquires, "How are you?"

"Old and sickly. And you?"

"I am not sure," Joshua says, as his eyes don't quite meet Yeshu's. "Troubled?"

Yeshu gives him a knowing look, full of empathy yet reluctance to have this conversation. "And what can I do to alleviate this?"

"You can begin by speaking plainly with me."

Yeshu looks at Joshua, a friend to him as well as once to his niece and the prophet. Slowly he shakes his head in support, knowing the time is long overdue to make an account of the passing years. "Then speak."

"Did you have to sell her to the palace?" Joshua pointedly asks him.

The older man takes a moment of silence except for a peculiar sound, as if holding back a welling of pain from his throat. He thinks back on the aftermath of Gomer's divorce. "God forgive me, I do regret it."

Ω

Within the ivory palace, from behind a veil, the King picks out Gomer from his harem. He commands in his piercing whisper, "She. The humble Goddess. The Prophet's wife."

Far from emotion, like a pagan image of the divine, she stands. Bejeweled in a cascading gold net of amber and emeralds hung from her neck and shimmering with gold paint brushed over her skin, she approaches his royal person. She will do what she must do, to please him in whatever he may wish.

Ω

Yeshu recalls the day he last saw his niece, after he had been dragged in front of their King's presence. "I begged for another price," he confides in Joshua. "Then I realized the King was not asking but demanding. It was Gomer went to him, or we both were to be destitute."

Joshua remembers the King taking over the means of olive oil production in all of Samaria, as the Ivory Palace was unable to keep pace with the Assyrians demand for it by paying the villagers for their output.

"The King would have taken even more," Yeshu continues. "He claimed what we had already been paid was merely a loan, and that's when he named that terrible price. Now I am waiting on this borrowed land for my last day, and it will not be long." He can no longer hold back his grief as he begins to speak through tears while his friend listens. "I used to joke with her that I could make a fortune selling her to the palace. And now I have truly done so, only for a roof over my head and a dwindling pantry. And the worst part is, she used to laugh with me when I said it. She would laugh," Yeshu says, trailing off into sobs.

"I am sorry," Joshua comforts him. "Thank you for telling me. You are not the only one to grieve these days. The King has taken much from all, in the name of appeasing this foreign army."

Gomer's uncle looks at Hosea's friend, recognizing forgiveness and understanding in his face. Yeshu then gains an amount of composure to ask about a troubled question that has gnawed him to the bone. "They were happy, were they not? My niece and the prophet. Against all odds, there was a time that they were happy."

"They were. And then they were not," Joshua replies.

"I know. They lost their son and then they were miserable."

Joshua makes a face as if he knows something he does not wish to say. But Yeshu does not notice.

"I do not go out much now. How has the prophet been since the divorce?" he asks Joshua.

"Worse than ever. All he does is preach woe."

Ω

Hosea stands tall above the people of Shomron, speaking in his impressive voice, "The Lord has divorced us. We are no longer his, we are no longer under his protection. Woe to the City on a Hill, for our destruction is coming. The Watchtower, Shomron, we are called. Now we only watch for the Assyrians, for our doom."

Ω

The two men, Yehoshua and Joshua, still sit in that home in the city, confessing to each other.

Yeshu laments, "I thought her being pregnant again would change things. That they might be happy with their daughter. But that is when they divorced. I could not understand, and my niece would never tell me why, even after she came back under my protection."

Now Joshua makes a sound of holding back a flood of grief. "I know why. It is what she told him when her daughter was born."

Ω

In the tent of their dwelling, after giving birth, Gomer hands a newborn girl to Hosea, and with the infant goes her mocking proclamation, "She is not yours."

Ω

Yeshu's eyes widen at this news. "Not his?"

"Yes," Joshua confirms.

"Then whose?"

The younger man takes a moment.

"Whose child is the girl?" Yeshu persists.

"I do not know," Joshua confesses. "She might still be Hosea's for all I know, and Gomer told me there were others, but she came to me…" he pauses. "The first time," he falters through his words, "I was stupid, she only wanted to hurt him. I thought I could console her, and she is so beautiful. I wanted her, I always did, and every time she came to me, I did not resist. God forgive me." Joshua looks at Gomer's uncle with tears in his eyes.

Yeshu collects himself. "It seems we have both sinned against those we love," he tells his friend.

They sit with each other, broken, yet both find solace in the other.

"Do you know anything of the girl? How old is she now?" Yeshu asks.

"She is four years of age. And she is lovely like her mother. I looked in on her once, while he was away. She lives with him, and he has an old woman care for her while he is gone preaching."

Ω

Hosea comes home to his dwelling place at evening time. The caretaker meets him outside and he dismisses her. Before entering his home, he takes out a bundle from his pack and uncovers a doll, a toy lamb, he bought at the market.

Ω

In the city, Yeshu sees Joshua out.

Just before leaving, his friend turns back to him. "The girl's name is Not-loved. But I refuse to believe there is any truth in it."

Ω

Hosea enters his tent while Not-loved draws pictures, ink smeared on her face and hands. She jumps and runs to him, making a mess of the parchment, and throws her body into his arms. "Papa," she shouts, gleeful at his return. He picks her up and holds her fast.

They share a meal of bread with olive oil and fish. Then he bathes her and laughs when she splashes him. Lastly, he puts her to bed, tucking her in with her new doll. As Not-loved falls asleep, he watches her face drift into unknown dreams. And then, he weeps.

Chapter Five

Another day, not long after his visit with Joshua, Yehoshua leaves the city on a donkey almost as old as he is. He travels down to the family tent that had once been his own, reigns in his beast of burden, and without getting down he calls out for the prophet.

Hosea exits the tent. "What is it you would have of me?" he questions with an abrupt voice.

"Words," Yeshu states. "Now would you be kind enough to help me off my ass?"

"That depends."

"On what?" Yeshu inquires, trying to remain patient.

"On what words you would have."

Yeshu thinks a moment before answering. "Of mercy and forgiveness."

"Who am I meant to forgive?" Hosea asks.

"You can start with me. For not coming before now. And I can forgive you for not coming to me. Whatever has happened, family should not be tossed aside."

Hosea remains unmoved.

Yeshu thinks his donkey is less stubborn than this man but decides to stay with his more humble and appeasing approach. "I have certainly come too late to have any moral high ground, but please do not send me on my way before letting me see my grandniece. Allow an old man a poor attempt at redemption."

After a hesitant moment, Hosea moves to help Yeshu off his mount. He then turns toward the tent and calls for Not-loved to come out.

Yeshu makes a sour face. "That name. Why would you—"

"It is what our Lord, Father has named us. We are Israel no longer, as he will no longer show us his love or forgive us."

"If God is the father, then that is a shit attitude. I suppose he finally tired of wrestling with his children."

Hosea passively glares at his past uncle-in-law, unimpressed by his clever attempt at a theological critique. "The Lord is holy and reproves how he sees fit; you may keep your blasphemies to yourself."

Hosea opens the front of the tent and calls out again. "Daughter, where are you?"

The two men hear laughing somewhere up above.

Not-loved sits in the branches of the old tree near the tent, hidden among the leaves.

"Come down," her father says.

"I cannot. Climbing up is easy. Climbing down without falling is hard."

Yeshu walks to the tree and stands directly under her. "Take hold of the branch in front of you."

Not-loved, with a scratch on her round and amiable face and her unkempt hair of dark curls falling from her head and breaking like waves onto her shoulders, curiously looks down on this old man beneath her tree. Then with care, she reaches out and grabs her new handhold.

"There," Yeshu encourages. "Now keep one foot where it is and slowly lower the other down."

"Okay." She puts her foot out into empty space.

"There is another branch under you," Yeshu directs.

"Where?"

"Move your foot around."

She finds the branch and sets her weight down on it.

"There you have it."

Then moving down another branch, and another, she jumps for the funny gray man to catch her. But she is intercepted by her father who grabs her from the open air and sets her down on the earth.

She looks up at Yeshu with inquisitive eyes. "Do I know you?"

"No, but I know you. I have helped your mother down from that tree before," he says with a fond and reminiscing smile.

Not-loved's face beams. "You know my mother?"

Yeshu would cry for remembering Gomer as his little niece, if he did not find her echo in the girl before him now so amusing. "Of course, I do. I am her uncle."

"Do you have any children?" she asks, hoping for a playmate.

Yeshu was never interested in marrying, and if he ever had wanted children, he had been satisfied and occupied with raising Gomer. "No, none of my own."

"Do you want to play with me?" she asks him.

He can think of nothing more in the world he would rather do. "Of course I want to play."

"I know," she begins with excitement. "I will pick flowers. Then we can weave crowns together." She runs off in search of flowers worthy of a coronation, leaving him with the prophet.

Watching her go, Yeshu asks, "What does she know of her mother?"

"Not-loved knows she is gone," Hosea answers.

Yeshu points, up the hill, to the city. "Not gone. She is still up there, waiting in the ivory palace to be acknowledged by those who belong to her. Would you deny your daughter her mother?"

"All she needs is her father."

"It is about being whole," Yeshu starts.

"Save me your—"

"I am talking about you. You are religious, fine. But you are trying something that does not fit. You love my niece, why fight that? Why break from her? Have mercy on yourself, have the grace to be wholly you," Yeshu rants, standing up to the prophet, though Hosea towers over him.

"I would rather be holy," Hosea insists.

"I thought only God is holy."

"Do not mince words with me, you know what I mean. I belong to the Holy Father, and that is all I wish."

Yeshu lets out his breath in exasperation. "Honestly, I do not know what you mean. I know you still love my niece. Is holy so far from being whole? Are you God's, only after burning everything and everyone away?" Yeshu points again, this time in

Hosea's face. "Then will you kindly leave the rest of us out of it and just immolate yourself for—"

Not-loved runs toward the two men. "Here, I picked them."

"Oh, thank you," Yeshu says, smiling, though he is red in the face. "I love them, like I love you."

"I love you too," she says. looking at him with the same bright amber eyes as her mother.

She is so innocent, Yeshu thinks. Then he wonders if she would still love him if she understood how he sold her mother, once to her father, the prophet, and then again to the King.

"Your great-uncle was just leaving," Hosea announces.

Yeshu grimaces. But then, he finds it best in this moment to concede against his wishes to stay. "I suppose I am. I am sorry, I will not be able to make that crown."

"It is alright. I can make it for you. You will come back for it, yes?"

"Even your father could not keep me away," he says, wishing it were true. "Now go pick more flowers, I'll need lots for my fat head."

Not-loved laughs and galivants back down the hill.

Yeshu turns to Hosea, while preparing to leave. "I do not care for your reasons why you sent my niece away. Go get her back from the ivory palace. She is so much more than a harem girl." As he mounts his donkey and begins his ascent back up the hill, Yehoshua has a vexing thought, that if by some miracle Gomer is redeemed from the King, how could he face her again after all that has transpired between them?

Ω

That night, the prophet is disturbed by a dream, an adamant voice calling out for him, "Anthropos."

"Hello? Who is there?"

"Anthropos."

He does not know if it is a whisper or a windstorm, but He recognizes the breath of YHWY. "Father? Yes, here I am." He stands and walks out of the tent, realizing it is not the tent of his home but of the famed Tabernacle of God. From out that place of holy dwelling, a great cloud of glory issues forth and is set alight as a pillar of fire in the sky. The guiding light then appears in the distance, as He follows it out into the wilderness, leading him into a honey-scented grove where the Ark of the Covenant awaits. As He approaches the flames disperse. And there, the voice of YHWY speaks from the seat of power between the two mighty cherubim raised atop the vehicle of God's presence. "Anthropos," the voice quakes, dwelling in the land, in the air, and in flesh.

"I am here, Father," He proclaims.

But then the voice changes, a subtle difference, as if gender could transform yet everything else remain the same. He knows it is no longer YHWY, it is now that of the Goddess, SHRH. "Anthropos is here."

Before He can surmise how He came to be in her presence, the two angels that cover the ark come to life and He now sees that one is male and the other female. They embrace and engage in sexual intercourse, as they begin to merge into one another, there at the Seat of God.

In dread, He shouts, "Father, save me from this profanity."

Then a great light is born from the two divine beings, and He is blinded.

"Help me. I cannot see," He pleads, with his hands stuck out in front of him.

Not-loved appears and takes his arm, leading him back to the Tent of the Tabernacle. She lets go at the entrance. "Here you are, but I can no longer be with you now."

"What do you mean?" He asks his daughter.

But there is no response as Not-loved is gone.

"My daughter? Where are you?" Again, no answer, only deafening silence.

Feeling his way into the Tabernacle, He finds there is nothing now but a vast emptiness. He staggers around the void, lost with no hope of escape. Then He stumbles over something. A block of stone, He thinks, as He lands in what feels like hot ash. "What is this place? Where am I?"

Then a new voice, Yehoshua, speaks to him, "It is your place. You made it."

"No, this is no place. It is nowhere and nothing is here," He howls.

"True. I am not here, too."

"I do not understand."

"You have denied the Mother," Yehoshua explains. "Without her, there is now no life born unto you. There is not even you."

And then, there is nothing.

Ω

"Daughter," Hosea cries into the darkness.

Waking into the womb of night from the dream, of which he still feels its presence of absence, Hosea frantically searches for Not-loved.

"Papa? Yes, here I am."

Hosea wraps his arms around her and holds her fast.

Ω

That morning, Hosea strides into the city with the first light of the sun, through the streets just now waking, and up the steps to the ivory palace. There, he is ushered into an audience chamber full of ivory trophies lining the walls, one being a full replica of the Ark. Hosea fights the urge to examine this, wondering if it fits the exacting dimensions of scripture. But the usher leaves him alone in the white and the waiting and Hosea turns his attention to the dais, veiled all around, which takes the prominent point of the room.

Hosea's wait passes interminably as he remains straight and tall, determined to be ready for this royal encounter, until a door opens, and Gomer enters in.

She wears a delicate silk skirt and is adorned in many gold circlets bracing around her limbs and clasping one great braid of her hair that snakes down to her calves. A dazzling necklace of amber and emerald caught in strands of gold pours from her neck and rests upon her breasts. Though she may be a slave she looks like a queen, stepping next to the platform.

Hosea must now contend with being in her burning presence. He did not expect to do this in front of her and almost buckles. Unable to bear the agony, he makes a movement, opens his mouth for a word, then is cut short from another presence hiding behind the veil.

"You have come to redeem her from me," the King states.

Hosea tries to discern the shape of the Veiled King beyond the thin wavering boundary. He does not like this ruler that perceives him yet hides from his own sight. And he now realizes that the King wanted him off his guard, with the shock of bringing her in for the deliberation, and that he quickly needs to gain his advantage. "I have."

"Yet you are the one who sent her away. Is it then your mistake you are correcting?"

"She sinned against the Lord and me. But as the Lord may show mercy, so may I."

"Mercy?" the King lets the word reverberate through the chamber. "Why withhold something so righteous and true only to bestow it later? God may have mercy, I do not rightly know, but men, they always have other reasons."

"However you may judge me to be, the fact remains, I am here to bring her back," Hosea asserts, reaffirming his purpose.

"For her own good, I am sure. You make it sound as if I have mistreated her," the King says, feigning wounded feelings.

Hosea knows he must be cautious with his words. "I have no doubt her needs are met. But she is more than a bed slave, even to a king."

"I see. More than a bed slave to a king, she is a bed slave to a prophet."

"A wife."

"I am amused by how you think there is a difference between what she is to me and what she is to you."

"With me, she—"

"Stop." The King parts the veil and steps down from his stage, bringing his presence fully into the room.

It is strange, he appears like Hosea but wears his royal hair long, and his face is shaven. His crown is ivory, and he is robed in ivory beads woven into peacock feathers. And his visage is painted like a heathen god or a woman. "She is valuable to me; I like having something that belongs to one such as you. Did you think I would just release her to you?"

"I am prepared to buy her back."

The King laughs, with a calculated coldness. "You sold everything to her uncle. And now I already own most of those holdings. So, prophet, you want to redeem her? With what?"

"With this." Hosea, doing his best to make a spectacle for the King, reveals from his robes his father's unicorn horn and astonishes the sovereign's face into a mask of envy and desire.

"It cannot be."

"It is," Hosea proclaims.

"How would you have come by such a mystery?"

Hosea answers, "My father traveled wide in his trades. It was a gift from some barbarian king of frozen seas." Then using his own voice of authority he calls out, "This is my payment. Do you accept?"

The King regains his composure from the sudden betrayal of his desire. He hates that he covets the treasures of this zealot, this man that preaches against his throne. But he never believed such a miracle as this truly existed. "You would give your very last for her. This fairy-tale touches my heart," he finally says. "But the real test is at home, not in grand gestures. Yes, I will take this payment of one of life's great mysteries in exchange for more of your woe together, man and woman. It seems to be ordained." He grabs the ivory horn from Hosea and slips back up the dais and into the royal shade projected on a sheet. There the King speaks once again from behind his veil. "Take her, she is restored to your side, once again as husband and wife."

He and She, together now but without word or glance, are escorted out.

Ω

Gomer, now dressed again in customary attire, leaves the city with her once-again husband. Though she still wears the jewels of the King's lust hidden underneath her robes. "A parting gift," the King had told her.

They left the city through the common western gate and now travel through the small villages of the southern slope, as they pass by a familiar plot of land, that once belonged to Hosea, and then Yehoshua, and now royal officials. Gomer reflects on walking this way with Hosea after their wedding years ago, realizing she is now in the same dilemma she was then. What will her life be, married to this man?

Approaching closer to their dwelling place, she stops as if a heavy barrier bars her way.

Hosea looks back behind him. "Come. Your home awaits you," he says.

"A moment, please," she gasps. Gomer gazes down the hill at her old home. An emotion mixed with longing and dread fills her soul and stays her body. "I am about to see my daughter, who is a stranger to me." Gomer has imagined her often. But she will not be that, she knows. She will be who she is.

"She is a kind girl and carefree," Hosea assures her. "She is full of love to give, though her name is Not-loved."

Gomer recoils at the name. She recalls Not-loved's birth, the agony and then sudden relief, a wave of euphoria. But after that she can't remember the warmth of holding her daughter, or the intimacy of feeding her from her breast. The only memory she has is telling Hosea her truth, wanting to hurt him, weaponizing the child. And she knew well the consequences, the laws of her people. Divorced from him, the child was solely his. "Appropriate, as I have been absent. A mother should be there to love her child."

Resuming the short journey, they come under the branches of Gomer's family tree when a slight girl with overwhelming joy and without patience comes running out from their home to her once-lost but now-found mother. The sight of innocent love overcomes Gomer, and she falls to her knees in tears as her own stranger daughter embraces her.

"Do not cry Mama. You are here, and I love you."

Gomer feels the warmth of Not-loved's body and her beating heart. She can smell the perfume in her hair. And she wants to say so much to her beautiful girl, this girl who in one gesture sets her free with unconditional love, after years of her own self-condemnation. But all she can muster are the words, "thank you."

"You are just in time," Not-loved says.

Is she just in time, Gomer wonders. So much has passed already. She wipes her tears and asks, "What am I in time for?"

"To play," Not-loved declares in a jubilant voice. "We can climb trees and make flower crowns. I have already made one for your uncle."

"My uncle." Gomer's feelings are complex. She hated her uncle for arranging this disastrous marriage, yet she turned to him after the divorce. She was angry with him for giving into the King's demand, though she knew there was nothing he could do, not really. The King would have taken her regardless, but perhaps Yeshu could have let it be a hill to die on, rather than live on in shame. Somehow though, she looks at Not-loved and remembers the love she still holds for the old man. "Is he still as careless and free as ever?" she asks her daughter.

"No. He seemed sad, like Papa. That is why he needs to play."

Hosea interjects, "Selling you to the palace was a burden he could not bear."

Gomer realizes now, her uncle must have had something to do with Hosea's decision to bring her back. In the presence of her child, her anger at old wounds is diminished. Right now, she is happy that this miracle of life, her daughter, is in her arms. She thinks that of all the wrong that came from her uncle and her husband, and this marriage, there is still this overwhelming love there in the person of Not-loved. "Perhaps, we could go and see him," Gomer tells her.

"Are we going now?"

"No," she answers, brushing the hair from her daughter's face. "It can wait for tomorrow. Today I only want to be with you. You are all that matters."

They enter together, mother and daughter, into the tent of dwelling. Hosea hesitates, and decides to stay outside, for them to be alone for a time.

Ω

That night, Hosea enters and sets a small meal of figs, cheese, and bread. Gomer and Not-loved draw pictures of themselves in their home but with improbable creatures, unicorns and something with two heads cartwheeling around. The more fantastic the harder they laugh. However, as they all eat together, a stillness and quiet sets in.

After dinner, Gomer sits beside her daughter, stroking her hair and caressing her to sleep. She glances across the tent to where Hosea has moved his bedding, thankful for the distance, and wonders at what being married again to this man means. She remembers how kind he was to her at the beginning of their bonds, and she remembers slowly being won over and giving into love for him. She reminisces all the times they fucked each other and is surprised when some small passion wakes in her now. But she recalls the unraveling too, and her husband's religious zeal, his madness. She then considers that maybe he plans on trying to woo her all over again, and muses, fleetingly, what if he has changed? Her husband looks over at her and she blows out her clay oil lamp then lays down, trying to turn her mind back to her sleeping daughter.

Peering across their home, Hosea gazes at his redeemed wife. He ponders over how he could express to Gomer his sorrow for abandoning her. He had let his anger take over when he sent her away, but now seeing her together with their daughter, he believes this is right. It is what the Lord, Father wants, reconciliation after discipline, he thinks. And then a revelation comes to him, that the Lord is showing him through his marriage, through his own family, the divine plan for Israel. This new vision invigorates him with purpose, and he goes to sleep, for once in a long time, with hope.

Ω

At dawn, in their dwelling place, Gomer rouses from slumber as Hosea readies himself for the coming day. "Are you going to preach?"

"I am."

"We will be in the city as well, visiting my uncle," she tells him. "You could come. For our daughter, we could try to be a family."

"Yes. For the sake of the Lord, we may be reconciled together. I can come to you when I am finished." He leaves her in the twilight with Not-loved still asleep by her side.

Ω

In the center of the city, that morning, Hosea prophesies to the Watchtower people. As always, he stands tall above the crowd and his voice can be heard over their clamoring. "I will tell you of the doom that is upon us, but I will also tell you of forgiveness. Though sins will be punished, the Lord may yet restore his people, as an unfaithful wife brought back into the home."

With the threat of Assyria and the King's overreach of control, more people follow the prophet around the city now, ready to hear his word of God. And as the woe Hosea preaches becomes more real every day, there seems to be more agreements and less curses from the gatherings. But today is different, today people hear a change in their dour prophet. While the woe remains, it is now partnered with a faith in the future, for salvation. And people begin to gather, to listen, and to hope.

Ω

Gomer and Not-loved take their time walking the city. For three years Gomer had not left the palace, and Hosea had seldom taken Not-loved here. Gomer avoids the royal grounds and the places her husband might be preaching but takes her daughter to the market where they breathe in all the earthy spices and indulge in delectable fruits, some sweet and others so sour they take turns tasting and crumpling their faces. As they go about their way, they get more than a few stares as Gomer catches what others say about her, the king's whore and the prophet's curse.

Then Gomer decides she can put it off no longer and must reconcile with her uncle. In truth, she misses him and the excitement of seeing him again takes over any misgivings. Approaching Yehoshua's home, they notice a small crowd gathered at his door. What kind of trouble has he done now, she wonders. She smiles, thinking of the mischief he might make in the city, as a guard ineffectually tries to dismiss the knot of people.

"What is happening here?" Gomer asks.

The city guard replies, "The occupant here has died, and we are trying to give the deceased's home some privacy while we look for his family".

The shock falls on her, numbing her mind and body. She hardly is aware of herself speaking to the guard, "I am his family, let me through." And all she hears are mumbles as the guard tries to warn her against looking in on the body without preparing herself.

She pushes past into the home then gasps and grabs Not-loved to her, burying the girl's face into her clothes. Yeshu is seated with eyes and mouth open as if ready to converse, as he ever was. But the eyes are glossed, and no whisper passes his hardened lips in that stone mask of what was once his jovial countenance. A ceremonial knife, used for sacrifice, the opened wrists, and the pool of blood is enough to tell the tale of her uncle's last story.

Ω

Among the growing throng of city-goers Hosea continues his prophesying. "We are, even now, under the knife of our own slaughter. The Lord has given us over to death. It is too late; our destruction is at hand."

Ω

In Yeshu's home, Gomer speaks to her daughter, keeping Not-loved's gaze focused on her. "My love. Turn and go, be brave and bring me back wash cloths. I will need many."

The girl turns and leaves without looking back. Gomer then closes the eyes of her uncle, bows his head, and sits down across from him.

Ω

"But forgiveness is never late," the prophet goes on. "Even after destruction, salvation may yet arise. Our children may see our fall, though there is hope for the future; forgiveness and reconciliation."

Ω

"Oh, God."

Hearing those words, Gomer looks up to see Joshua, the man she once used to hurt her husband.

And Joshua then notices her, Gomer's presence coming upon him as a second hit of pain, after the sight of Yeshu. "You are here," he plainly states.

"Sorrow is my abode, so of course I am here. You are here as well."

Joshua walks further in, trying not to glance at his dead friend. Nodding, he says, "I look in on your uncle, from time to time."

"A fraternity of men in my life," Gomer confirms.

"I am sorry."

"Do not be. I thank you for keeping him company."

Joshua shakes his head trying to be more precise, "I am sorry for more. I am sorry for—"

Gomer does not want to hear it. "Help me with the body please, before my daughter returns."

Ω

"Our wrongs may be made right again," Hosea ends his preaching. The crowd murmurs as some ask when doom will come, or how their salvation will be worked out. As always, they want material answers and not spiritual. But Hosea has a duty to his family and leaves the flock with their questions.

Ω

Not-loved, with red and swollen eyes downcast, brings in an armful of rags. She stands there without looking up. Then she almost retches from the strange smell in the room, like rotten eggs and oversweet grapes.

Gomer speaks to Joshua, as she fills a basin with water from the home's cistern. "If I may ask another favor of you, will you take my daughter out and occupy her?"

He takes Not-loved by the shoulders and escorts her out while Gomer begins to clean the body of her uncle.

"Come on," Joshua says. "I will buy you a date at market. I know who sells the sweetest ones."

Despondent, as they leave, Not-loved merely acknowledges, "But I have already been to market."

With them gone, Gomer focuses on wiping away the cascade of blood covering his wrists and hands, revealing raw purple gashes. She rinses out the rags, mixing the blood and the water. And she sobs. And then she screams. "How dare you do this. You stole from me my anger. You coward," she begins to berate him. "You always found a way out. A way to make me laugh or pity you, so my fury would abate. You always wanted my love, but always on your terms, you could never bear anything else from me. No, I will not let you do this, not this time. I hate you for always taking the easy way out. I cannot forgive you." But she continues to care for the body, as she had cared for the man in life.

Ω

Joshua and Not-loved are together at the market, where Hosea happens upon them and calls out for his daughter. On his way to the city home, news of Yeshu's death has already reached him. He kneels before Not-loved and takes care to study her face. "Are you okay," he asks, but already knows she is not, while he listens to her lie that she is fine.

Joshua, unsure of how to be around his once friend, awkwardly waits to take cue from how Hosea reacts to his presence.

Hosea chooses to ignore the fact of his former friend's being. He stands, taking Not-loved by the hand. "Come, let us take care of your mother."

Before they walk away, Joshua decides to break through his feigned lack of existence. "I have this date for her."

Hosea, without looking back, states, "My daughter needs nothing from you."

Not-loved though turns around and manages a smile. "It is okay, friend. You keep it."

Hosea takes his daughter from the market, leaving Joshua alone. With a stern look, he tells her, "That man is not our friend."

Ω

At sunrise the next morning, Hosea pushes a cart carrying the bier of Yehoshua back and forth across the way of the dead, a narrow path cut into the steep eastern face of the watchtower hill. Gomer and Not-loved walk behind. Halfway down, where the shadows of twilight still linger, a small tomb, among many small tombs carved from the hillside, waits to receive Yeshu like a reverse stone womb. There the body is laid. And, as his mourners step back, the light of the rising sun shines upon the dead, chasing away the remaining shades and coloring the death-shrouds with the fire of life, like an ineffectual resurrection.

Chapter Six

In the dwelling place of He and She, after a long day of laying their uncle to rest, Gomer sits beside her sleeping daughter, Not-loved. From across the large family tent, she watches her husband reading by lamplight on his own bedding.

Catching her stare, Hosea sets aside his preoccupation and looks back at that face full of grief. "I am sorry," he says.

Something roils in her: despair, regret, anger. She needs someone to comfort her, to love her. She needs someone to touch her. She makes an expression as if almost loosing a torrent of emotion before catching it back. Then, sudden and swift, her body leaps in one motion across the space between them and on top of Hosea, where she takes hold of him with her hand to stiffen him.

"No," Hosea meekly protests.

"I need this," she says with her under-skirt hiked about her waist and pulling off his linens.

Hosea whispers, "Not now." He glances at their daughter, still in a slumber.

"Quietly; slow, and we won't wake her," Gomer entices, as she bends down to kiss him. Then she pushes his shoulders to the ground, and with her hands on his chest she sits up straight, with him between her legs but not yet within. With measured movements, she begins to slide over him, back and forth and side to side in a circle.

Hosea's eyes are shut as he feels the slick heat of Gomer's body washing over him. But then, as Gomer just begins to bring him up into her, he peers upon her countenance, to discover her mouth wantonly open as she gazes down at him. He is suddenly alarmed by her eyes, round and shining in the night like the predatory lilith. Pushing her off, he commands, "I said, not now."

Gomer freezes there momentarily, downcast and stone-faced, then creeps back to her place beside Not-loved. Still and quiet, she hides a soul stirred into a tempest.

Hosea looks again at her, wanting to give her what she desires, yet is afraid that it would not console but only inflame the flesh. Healing comes from the Lord, he silently insists to himself. And turning his face from her, he tries to sleep.

Ω

In the morning, after Hosea leaves, Gomer wakes Not-loved and they break their fast together. The young girl, usually bright-faced and exuberant, remains gloomy since the death of her great-uncle, and after eating she walks outside to sit under her mother's tree.

Left alone, Gomer halfheartedly rummages through Hosea's papers and practices her writing. When she takes up the small black well, ink spills at her wrist and pours down like blood from an open vein. With hurried determination, she attempts to fashion a form from the chaos, writing with her finger along her arm one word: beloved. She weeps.

Ω

As the sun begins to fall from its pinnacle, Hosea too descends toward home. He wanders down the great hill from the walled city of Shomron, into the tent of their dwelling, and finds

Gomer waiting for him, their daughter gone. "Where is Not-loved?"

"I sent her to your widowed caretaker."

Hosea observes something wild in Gomer's countenance. "Why?"

So he cannot use her as an excuse, she thinks. And then to the point, she demands, "Fuck me."

Hosea tries to explain his hesitance, "No. If we can wait until—"

"I need to be fucked," she stands in front of him, absolute in her sensuality.

Hosea responds with an emphatic, "No."

Gomer's exasperation with her husband grows. She needs to feel close to someone. After Yeshu's death, she needs to feel alive. "Why did you bring me back here?"

Hosea searches for a reason. "Redemption." And then he charges, "I paid a high price."

How dare he use that against her, she thinks. And she challenges him, "You bought me back like cattle after sending me away."

"You wanted to go."

"Because your love had already gone," she yells out, her body strained.

Hosea is at a loss. He tries to understand the sorrow she bears but does not understand her aggression toward him. He saved her from enslavement to an earthly king, he thinks. "What is it you want of me?"

"I want you to love me," she says with desperation. "All of me, as I am. But I will settle for you fucking me."

"Love you? I came after you and brought you out of that shameful place."

"Yes, it was shameful," she shouts, nodding her head in agreement. "This too is shameful," she then says, pointing at him. "For a woman it is all prostitution, lowering yourself to please your husband or lord, like men are higher beings." She laughs, high and ringing, with sudden revelation and declares, "Of course. That has always been the truth. You think you are my lord, you want to be the Lord, to be the same as God."

"Ridiculous," he denies. "Oneness with the Lord is not a thing to be grasped, it is enough to know the Lord."

A faraway look grows in Gomer's eyes as if she is looking past Hosea. To know, she considers. And then, musing aloud, she says, "We can never really know anything but ourselves. To know is to be." And a question comes from deep within her being: Is that where they falter? Do they not know theirself, who they are? Her awareness of here and now returns, as she looks upon the material presence of her husband. "You say you believe in mystery, yet you believe truth must be dictated."

Hosea turns to pedantry. "It must be dictated because it belongs to the Lord, and it is a mystery because the Lord is apart from us, his presence separated out in the Temple, the Holy Place, and the Holy of Holies," he says.

"Why must God be separated so?" Gomer asks, wondering, why all these ridiculous rules? Then, with each question fiercer than the last, she inquires, "What if there was no Holy of Holies? What if the veil was torn open and the Holy was poured out for everyone; what if the Temple was broken and God was handed out everywhere? What if God was even here, in this woman speaking with you now, suffering from desire and despair?"

Where does this heresy come from, Hosea ponders. First, she accuses him of wanting to be God, then muses about being

God herself. As if God, the Highest, from where all law and authority emanates, could even lower enough to dwell in humanity. She does not know what she says. She describes nothing but anarchy. It is fearful. "You might as well ask for the death of God," he exclaims.

A temporary silence falls after emotions flare.

Gomer takes a breath. "When you came for me, I thought this was a new chance to be one with you. Again, I ask why? Why did you bring me back here?"

"I thought saving you might change you," he cries.

Gomer allows this telling statement to fall upon her person. The burden is borne for a moment, then as she sees through it, she lets it fall to the dirt. It is not her he wants, she perceives, but merely an idea of her, his ideal subservient in her body.

Hosea notices her thinking, mistaking it as a sign in his favor, and presses further. "I want who I know you are meant to be."

Gomer knows this place, where no ground is given. "Will you not fuck me?"

He hesitates. Would it be so wrong to give her this little bit of fleshly comfort, a moment of pleasure for a passing reprieve of pain? He wants her as well. Even through his anger, he has desired her these past four years. No, he decides, he must remain steadfast, so that they may both increase with the strength of YHWY. "Not now. Wait. Let us first grow together in the wisdom of our Lord."

"Grow into who I am meant to be?" In her heart, Gomer asks SHRH for strength.

"Yes," he replies.

"I can grow."

Hosea exhales with relief. He realizes how tense she has made him. "Yes. Please. Let us break this animosity between us."

Another silence falls. And as she begins to form a vision of just how she will grow, another question comes to Gomer, one she had not considered before and is unsure why she wonders just now. "Do you really believe destruction for Shomron, for Israel, is coming? A true end?" she asks.

Hosea studies her face and thinks upon the prophecies he's received of destruction and doom. He wonders, can they still be one, be together at the end? Can they again find love and joy in each other, as everything burns around them? "I have seen it," he answers.

Ω

One morning, not long after, Hosea exits the tent of their dwelling to find Gomer already going about her morning duties. They work the olive press together, then he fills up a cart to receive rations for their quota. Afterward, he is startled by laughter and turns to watch his wife and daughter play together around the large matriarchal tree of theirs; of Not-loved's, of Gomer's, and of their maternal ancestors'.

Later, as the day darkens, Hosea enters their home to find it cleaned, supper laid out, and Not-loved washed. They eat their meal together and then Gomer urges for her and Not-loved to listen to Hosea read the scriptures and for them all to beseech the Lord in prayer as a family.

The night grows, and he watches her by lamplight put their daughter to bed. "Today was a good day," he says, thanking her.

"I am growing. You will see."

Taking her by the hands, he moves in to gently kiss her goodnight.

But slyly, she pulls away. "Wait. Even this small gesture might be too much for me now."

"Do not worry, beloved. We will wait till the time is right," he assures her. But he wonders if by the power of the Lord she is not already restored, marking the change in her demeanor. "Tomorrow evening, why don't you hire Not-loved's caretaker for the night and we may keep each other company, and speak encouragement to one another."

Gomer's eyes shine at this proposal, and later she bathes herself where he can see. And he does watch her, and she knows, and she smiles a smile for herself, hidden away from him.

That night, as her family sleeps, Gomer slips outside the tent of their dwelling, into the dark, and down the hill, to the sweet fig-scented groves where she finds the Priestess. The sacred woman is undressed and wading waist-deep in a stream, having just ministered to one of her flock, those of the city that seek out her rites of ecstasy in secret. Gomer waits for her to clothe herself in the night-deep purple robes and hood of her profession. "Please, I have need of your craft once more."

The shrouded woman listens intently to Gomer's desires, then wanders through the shadows under the trees, gathering to herself pungent and resinous herbs of the wild.

Ω

The next day, Hosea comes home from preaching in the city to find the old caretaker, waiting with his daughter and a lamb.

"A gift from your wife. Eat, then wash." The widow woman hands over the innocent animal and takes Not-loved into her care.

He slaughters the lamb, hangs it from a branch, then cooks and eats a portion of the flesh, thankful for this gracious gesture, and already hopeful that tonight they may be reunited fully with each other. Although he quickly checks his anticipation, wishing first to speak with his wife.

After washing at the water basin set outside the entrance of their dwelling place, Hosea enters as the sun first sets. Inside, the large familial tent has been rearranged. He is in a room filled with light from a large seven-mouthed lamp and clouds of incense, with a curtain drawn before him on four wooden pillars, separating out an inner room from his own place of waiting. From behind this veil a voice issues forth, "Take off your sandals and wait on me."

He does as She says, then sits and partakes of bread and wine laid out before him. Another kind service, He thinks, already forgetting his worries. Waiting within the cloud, He breathes in the perfumed and intoxicating smoke, a familiar smell of piney-sweet frankincense yet masking a pungent musk He cannot place. As his thinking slows, his more basic instincts sharpen, sensing the material world around him in a new and exciting way. Hazily, He begins to wonder if this is a dream, then is interrupted by her voice, ordering him, "Remove your clothes and enter."

Standing up slow, as his head swims, He disrobes and then penetrates through the veil, into an even thicker cloud of presence. She is here, though He does not perceive her yet in the dark and smoke, having left the light of the lampstand. He gropes for her.

"I am here," She calls to him. Materializing from the swirling cloud around her, She reveals her form born from the dark, and, completely losing himself to her, He embraces her body with immediacy and eagerness.

Giving him a taste of her parted lips, She then presses away and commands, "First, drink full from my cup." And laying back on a raised bed of furs and pillows She directs him downward, and He places his gaping and thirsty mouth between her legs, gorging on her sweet libation, and grasping her waist as She begins to writhe.

She knows now, He is hers for the night. And as her ecstasy takes over her in waves, She falls onto her side and pulls herself around to take the horn of his hard flesh into her own mouth, as together they become a circle of one entwined.

But before He can reach release, She remembers herself. "Enough." She stands and takes him up by the hand. "Follow me." Leaving the dark cloud, they pass through the light of the lampstand and into the night where the waxing moon rides high in the sky. The pillar of cloud seems to follow them, as She leads him down below the kingly hill of Shomron and into the pagan groves. "Now. Fuck me," She orders, finding her own amplified voice of authority.

Naked, as the first man and woman in the beginning, He and She fuck each other under the trees. They stand together, as She is leaned over, her hands pressed against a trunk, its rough texture matching and adding to her pleasure. He moves inside her, seizing her from behind, with a wild rapture. And with release He fills her with his seed.

But She is not done, and turning to face him, She presses him onto the ground. Then, on top of him, She brings them both together to climax. A climax for not only She and He, but for the whole of being, from the first of humanity to the last, and even for the godhead, as with He, She unifies the once sundered God and Goddess within their body.

And as He melts into She, He feels himself as female and She as male, her self penetrating into his. Then slipping further, shedding their skins and all they knew to be them, they cease even to be human. Driven only by hunger and instinct they become all that swims, flies, and creeps along the Earth, until changed again into rooting things, their essence falls into the underworld as one dead, before a sudden light takes them and their unified round celestial body bursts into innumerable sparks out among the stars of heaven.

Yet, all this was only a passing infinity, as of things that might be, found in one fixed moment of desire.

Ω

In the mixing of twilight, He and She are asleep, after their passion at the edge of the wilderness. She remains astride him, and their genitals are still connected. As the sun rises, a wind blows through the trees and a voice speaks, "Anthropos."

Breathing in the honeyed air, Hosea opens his eyes. Knowledge comes rushing in, sobering and unclouding his mind, and he sees his nakedness. Then, disentangling himself from his wife, all in a rage, he stands up in the grove. "What is this that you have done?"

"I have made you mine, if only for one night," she answers.

"You have defiled me," he roars. "You brought me here, to fuck in the grove of the goddess, like heathens. After all I have done. What am I to do with you?"

"Nothing. You want to embody YHWH so badly, you want to be He," she explains with ferocity. "Fine, then I am She, his and your disgraced Queen of Heaven, once the Mother of All, now the Whore of Sheol. I am the cost of your pride, your great arrogance that you cannot share the divine light, not even with I, your so called beloved."

"I will no longer have you in my home," he declares so forcefully that his voice grows hoarse. "You are banished from my presence."

"I am home," she proclaims. "I will stay here among the trees and be a priestess of SHRH. And I will bear you more children of my divine infidelities, as I know the King atop the Watchtower Hill will not acknowledge another divorce."

Hosea rushes off in anger, as Gomer laughs and begins to dance free and naked among the trees in the light of the dawning sun.

Ω

Passing up the hill, onlookers gawking at his nudity, Hosea reaches the place of his dwelling and dresses himself in sackcloth. Then he pauses as his eyes go to the great tree that has constantly stood beside him, that has always belonged to her. He begins to cut down all the smaller trees from his plot of land and builds up the brush around the trunk of that old family tree of hers. And setting fire to the kindling, he watches as the flames grow and darken the trunk, licking upward at the branches and charring the carcass of the hanging lamb.

Late in the day, the trunk weakens, and the wizened tree falls over, tearing the place of dwelling open as the fabric of the tent catches fire. Then, in the last of the day's light, as the fire burns to embers, Hosea walks into the desolation, taking only a handful of ashes from what has been his residence and anoints himself with those remains.

Ω

Down the great watchtower hill, as Hosea seethes in the glow of a dying light, Gomer, now a silhouette in the maternal night, patiently waits in the grove, when the Shrouded Priestess comes to her.

She leads Gomer into one of her many hidden hollows, as the moon rises. There the Priestess makes a fire and lets the shroud fall from her body. In the firelight, she appears strikingly like Gomer, yet slighter, and with a shaved head, not unlike some men. However, what sets her uniquely apart from the men and women of Israel and Judea is a tattoo of a serpent coursing along her spine. The tail coils at her sacrum, the body twists up around blooms likened to an Egyptian waterlily, and its jaws reach to the top of her head, connecting the two great tetragrammatons of Goddess and God, root to crown.

The Priestess takes a stone with a depression carved out in the shape of a woman and sets it onto her fire. As the rock heats, she mixes a batter, and the woman of the Goddess pours this into the mold.

"Is there truly a God and Goddess?" Gomer asks.

"The divine is separated from their self," the Priestess answers. "Being one with God, being one with another, being one and whole in yourself; it is all just one. Even the sacred and the profane are the same. But we have forgotten the Goddess, we have forgotten ourselves, we have forgotten the holy whole."

"Is all belief and religion only riddles?"

"It is life. And life is mystery. If you are to partake of the mystery, you must be born again through the Goddess." The Priestess hands a cake, in the form of woman, from the hot stone to Gomer. "Take, eat, this is her body."

APOCALYPSE

Another Interlude

Inside her family's city home, Not-loved, now ten years old, cleans up after having eaten breakfast. She then sits with Not-mine, her two-year-old brother, as they play with an old doll, a toy lamb years ago singed by fire, when a visitor arrives at the entrance. A familiar voice calls out.

"Come in, friend," she says, welcoming Joshua.

He enters, as handsome as ever, now with a dusting of white scattered through his dark hair and lines at the corners of his eyes. He sits by the low table and hands Not-loved a bowl of dried fruit, nuts, and stale bread. Looking over the girl, tall for her age and with a lean, knowing face full of cares, he briefly recalls the once round cheeked and carefree child. Though he acknowledges the one thing that has not dimmed in her, her innocent way of kindness and love.

"Sorry it is not as much as last time," he laments about the food. "There is less and less coming into market each day." He knows the reason there is not enough food, as the Assyrians have seized most of the surrounding lands of Samaria over the last several years and now gather their strength in the mountains near the hill of Shomron. And he knows that Not-loved knows, yet he still chooses not to discuss their impending doom with her.

"It is enough for Not-mine and me."

He winces, looking from the boy to the girl. "Why do you insist on using that name, as well as your own?"

"He is Not-mine and I am Not-loved." The boy, with a red face and close-cropped black hair sits in his sister's lap, looking up at her with deep brown eyes. "Those are our names; they and this home are all we have."

Joshua decides not to press the matter further, instead asking a question he has meant to ask many times before. "Do you see your father often?"

"When he preaches, he is hard to miss."

Ω

Hosea stands amidst a crowd, dressed in rough hair-cloth and a raw leather belt. He is unkempt and wild, his body used to rooting down into the soil and curling around rock. His hair is grown out, and yet his graying beard is cut nearly to the skin of his face, kept this way in penitence. "Do not trust in the walls of your Watchtower City," his still booming voice rings out. "They will fall, and the city will burn. All that is left is to witness the end. We are the last watch of the House of Joseph."

Ω

Joshua knows what she means. With the threat from the Assyrians obvious to everyone now, Hosea's preaching draws out almost the whole of Shomron. "I meant, do you spend time with him?"

"Father comes by, though not as much as Mother. I do not know what he eats, because he always refuses our food, just as he refuses to sleep here. But he will bathe here sometimes. I even had him change his sackcloth not long ago. If there is anything you need from him, you can usually find him residing just outside the northern city wall. He likes to be an eyesore to the King's Road travelers."

"No, I need nothing. Only curious." Joshua breaks from his questioning while the girl and her small brother take some bites. Short from living here, he has seen after the children increasingly more through the years as their parents' religious devotions grew, even mirroring the estrangement and neglectfulness of their God and Goddess. Though he admits to himself he too is careful of avoiding Gomer and Hosea, making sure he is not around when they do come to visit their children. "How is your mother?"

"Better than Father. She will stay with us on occasion. She brings us money she receives from grateful devotees."

Ω

After ministering, Gomer bids blessings to one of her faithful. Her hair is cut and plaited in numerous braids that fall around her shoulders. Her face and body are painted in vibrant colors of blue, purple, and scarlet. And even in her nakedness, she remains clothed in precious jewelry, offerings from satisfied lovers, that glitters along with her shining amber eyes. Where the Priestess has made use of a more discreet aesthetic, Gomer has embraced a flamboyant abandon. Her body, no longer in the easy bloom of youth, still evokes the image of the Goddess, arousing worshipful passion from those who seek her out.

Walking to a cold spring, she immerses herself in the pool's depths, washing away her recent religious duties. She then dries herself in her clean and rocky hollow and lays aside a gift of gold coin beside the other belongings she shares in common with the Priestess. Perusing the small hoard, she picks up a dagger made from a strange metal, its handle fashioned in the shape of a wanton woman. She remembers the peculiar man who gifted it to her.

He was from far away and paler than anyone she had seen before. But he knew her language enough to claim Gomer's likeness after some foreign goddess of his own, one of love and beauty. He described in poetry that Gomer was that bright star of the morning, bringer of light, and of the evening, fallen to earth. And he had said the dagger itself was wrought from a fallen star and therefore rightfully belonged to her. She had been so smitten that she then attended to him a second time, without need of any further offering.

Carefully, she lays the dagger back down and then lays herself down on her bedding to rest. But before she can close her eyes, she hears a voice call out from the edge of the wilderness, "Priestess of the Goddess, Queen of Heaven and Mother to All. I have come to the sacred grove to taste her sacred fruit."

She walks back toward the honey scented trees and answers the summons with a question. "And what is her name?"

Ω

Not-loved thinks on the curious nature of her parents. Somehow it happened that most of her life, here in this home, she was raised by her father during the warm and blooming season, as that time belonged to her mother in the groves. But during the wet and cold season her mother would stay in the city with her, while her father would live as a vagrant, preaching among the biting and barren stones.

However, this past year, her mother brought a brother to stay in the home and then returned to the sacred trees after weaning him. Both parents then drifted to a more impermanent presence in their lives, looking in on them sporadically, Father and Mother becoming more and more identical to their divine counterparts. But as their time at home lessened, her friend has replaced them both as a stable adult help, while she has learned to daily parent herself and her brother. "Both will always do the same thing before coming in," Not-loved says of her parents.

"What is that?" Joshua asks.

"They ask first if the other is here."

"They still refuse to be in each other's presence?"

She looks at him as if to say, do you do any differently? Instead, she replies, "In six years I doubt they have been able to completely avoid the other, but their faces are certainly turned away so that they do not see. I do not know if they have ever really known—"

Not-loved is interrupted by horns blowing. Deep horns that jar and shake, horns that could wake the dead, and though not unexpected, now still surprise with dread. For a moment, Joshua and Not-loved are frozen, then she forcibly breaks the spell, speaking aloud the truth no one wants to hear, "They are coming."

Joshua embraces both children, unsure if the rest of the day will last.

Ω

Outside the city wall, atop the great Watchtower Hill, Hosea stands up as the warning horns echo through the city behind and are answered by horns of war suddenly carried up by a great wind. He looks out at the surrounding mountains as their bodies tremble, their trees churning in the sudden gale. Then he sees what the wind has brought, a deluge of fire and forged iron, streaming through the forests and into the valley. He turns, and as the gates begin to shudder, he directs those nearby to safety and follows them into the city.

Chapter Seven

Gomer is stirred by the sound of the war horns flowing over the wilderness. She stands upright onto her feet and runs out to the edge of her grove. There she sees soldiers, with the light of the morning sun glinting off their scale armor, descending like flashes of lightning toward the hill of Shomron, and holding firebrands in their hands.

The Priestess appears beside her.

Remembering all the prophecies of doom her husband preached, Gomer asks her superior, "He was always right, was he not?"

The Priestess answers, "Anyone who did not know the Assyrians were always coming here is a fool."

"I meant about it being the end," Gomer states, watching the end of her world unfold.

"The Omega is always with us," the Priestess elucidates, as she takes Gomer's hand. "As is the Alpha. The whole story is there, in every word. And an apocalypse is only a revelation for a new beginning." The Priestess delivers Gomer her strange dagger. "They are coming. Go to your family, before your path is cut off from you."

"What about you?" Gomer worries.

"They are men, like all men. And I will wait for them here as I always have."

"Please, come with me. You do not want what they have for you."

"No, I do not. But going behind the walls will only delay it and allow fear to grow stronger. I do not have a family to comfort me as you do. You must leave, now."

With haste, Gomer ties a skirt up above her knees and drapes herself in the great purple cloak of her sisterhood, girding it around her waist with a crimson sash and secreting the dagger away in a hidden pocket. Then she runs to the foot of the hill and up, always moving her way around from sight of the encroaching army but ultimately losing as the horde of soldiers tightens its grip around the western and northern sides of the hill.

As she nears the city, she falls in step with other village outliers, field workers and poorer families. Together, they all run from the advancing enemy line and toward the great north gate. But there, they find it already barred and refusing to open, even as the people cry out for salvation. For a moment Gomer wonders at the giant wooden doors, their carved celestial lovers now locked in embrace. What does this herald? The question is evoked in Gomer, as Hosea, unbidden, enters her mind's eye. She can see him searching for her amid flames.

But as the army rises toward the doors, cutting down many at the edge of the crowd, some of those nearer the wall run toward the east and Gomer follows, leaving behind her vision. In a panic, searching for escape at the narrow path above the way of the dead, those ahead again discover to their dismay that it is already blocked by rubble. This having been done by the city guards as a defensive measure. Some try to clamber over but are shot down by a barrage of arrows. And running now to nowhere, Gomer is caught in a stampede and her own fear, as all flee toward a precipice and over the edge, falling into the trees below.

Ω

Hosea walks into his old family home to find Not-loved, Not-mine, and Joshua waiting an excruciating wait. Not-loved looks up at her father and runs to him, throwing her arms around his neck.

"Be strong my daughter," Hosea comforts her. "Remember that whatever happens, it is the Father's will."

"But what should we do now?" she asks. "This waiting is unbearable."

"I will go and hear what the King has to say. He should have a plan for the people, then I will return to you." Hosea kisses Not-loved's forehead and adds, "But first I will find soldiers to send you. They will want to guard our door." He turns to leave but then looks back at Joshua holding Not-mine. "Watch over them."

"I will."

Hosea leaves and Joshua wonders at the man's calm demeanor, and how Hosea even seemed grateful that he was there with the children. Then with realization, he looks at Not-loved and comments, "He did not ask."

"Ask what?"

"He did not ask if your mother was here, before coming in."

"Oh God, Mother," she exclaims, her eyes widening with concern. "She should have been here by now."

Ω

Gomer opens her eyes. Confused, she stares through branches convulsing in the wind, though it is not the sky she sees through them, but the ground. Then she remembers her fall and losing consciousness in the air. Taking a moment to breathe into her body, she determines her injuries. She is bruised all along one side where she was caught in tight-knit brush, a sharp ache radiates down the arm that broke her fall, and blood seeps from somewhere on her head. But she can move, and the adrenaline rushing through her fills her with impatience for pain. Disentangling herself, she climbs down the tree that cradles her.

A few others were lucky enough to have found a safe landing, but most of those who went over the cliff only careened through the canopy to land broken on the rocky ground below. And the Assyrian army, still assaulting from the north-west, has yet to circle this far around the hill, where it is the wildest, thick with forest beneath a steep eastern face. Those that survived the fall now take advantage of their opportunity, running into the wilderness away from Shomron forever.

All but Gomer, who now looks at the narrow path cut back and forth across the cliff and up to the eastern wall. It is the way of the dead, that winds past the tombs hollowed into the rock for The Watchtower City's deceased. It is the way she took when she put her uncle to rest six years ago, and it is her only path open to her now, as she begins her serpentine way, among the dead of Shomron, and up to the City on a Hill.

Ω

In the city, four young Shomron men enter the home as Joshua looks them over. They do not even have proper armor, only hardened leather, he judges. And studying one in particular, Joshua deems him not much more than a boy, as he shyly stands staring at the ground. "We were expecting soldiers," he bemoans.

The oldest of them answers, "We are in training."

"And I suppose you are the best they would spare," Joshua says with a sigh.

"So. What should we do?" another asks.

Joshua shrugs then points to the back room with the door built into the wall. "You are here to guard. There is the door. Guard it."

Ω

Halfway up the way of the dead, Gomer looks down to see the first Assyrian scouts begin their way after her. Moving fast, they use light ladders to climb straight up from pathway to pathway, instead of walking the winding way back and forth. She tries to keep low and cling to the cliff, hoping they have not yet seen her. Then she stops, discovering she is beside the tomb of her uncle, Yehoshua.

Stealing another glance down past her foot path, Gomer acknowledges that she will not win the top before she is overtaken. So, she hides in her uncle's tomb underneath his linen-wrapped corpse. From there she watches the trampling feet of the soldiers run by, but soon struggles to breathe, as the burial smells of resin and herbs over corruption become overpowering. Straining to hear, she determines the footsteps have moved far enough away. And breathless, she crawls out from under Yeshu's body.

Back upon the path, gasping in air, she looks up at the assailants, and witnesses them shooting arrows alight with fire at the defenders above the wall. However, this small group of Assyrian scouts are quickly dealt with by the guards' bolts and stones loosed down atop their heads.

Thinking her way now clear, she stands. Then she hears someone speak to her in a language she does not know. Surprised, she turns around to find another scout behind her as he lays down his bow with an arrow already lit and takes out a long knife. As the soldier approaches, Gomer stumbles back into the shallow tomb. The Assyrian raises his knife above her. But then, thinking she has only put her hands up in defense, Gomer looks and instead finds her strange dagger of the wanton goddess clasped by both her hands and its sharp blade buried in the soldier's belly. The man looks confused and then suddenly the shadow of her would-be killer leaves from over her, as a stone careening down the way of the dead finds its mark, crushing his skull and sending his body back down to the ground.

Still holding the dagger, Gomer stares at it and thinks it a miracle she still had it on her after her fall. Putting it away, she steels her nerves to keep moving when a great rending sound of doom shakes the hillside. Looking up again, she finds that the guards on the wall have all moved away. And she realizes that the city gate has fallen to the enemy.

A war horn blows from the north and is answered from just below Gomer, where she spies more of the Assyrian army moving around the hill and through the trees, many of them carrying ladders. She gazes one last time upon the shrouded corpse of her uncle and thanks him with a silent prayer. Then she drags him out onto the narrow path. After moving more bodies from their tombs, Gomer begins to break open pots of incense and embalming fluids, soaking the ledge behind her. Then, using the soldier's burning arrow, she sets it all alight. The wind blows, fanning the flames, and baptizes the way of the dead in fire.

Finally, Gomer gains the straight path under the eastern wall and, running south, she turns the corner with the low stone fence of her husband's family land in sight. But another sight turns her victory to dread as she witnesses the vast might of the Assyrian army, now completely encircling the foot of the great Watchtower hill, cutting off any hope of escape.

Ω

In front of the Ivory Palace, Hosea finds a large group of citizens gathered, but the King remains shut inside without word. He begins to move around the crowd to take a small alleyway on the side of the great pale building, when a young boy grabs his arm. "Prophet, you told us this would happen. I am sorry I played with the asherim pole, am I going to die because of that?"

"Have faith in our Lord Father and stay with your family," he tells the boy. "The King may yet have a word for us." Hosea leaves and finds the side entrance he was looking for but is surprised to find no guard and even more surprised to find the door open to him.

Ω

Joshua and Not-loved are playing a game. They draw nonsense characters like a winged snake eating its own tail and a two-headed person, trying to make Not-mine laugh, trying to keep their minds off the imminent threat, when a pounding is heard in the home.

"They are at your father's door," Joshua mourns.

The three of them huddle together in fear, but then Not-loved looks up with renewed hope. "Wait, listen."

Joshua picks up his head and listens to the sound outside the wall, discerning cries for help.

"Mother," Not-loved calls out.

Joshua stands. "Stay here." He runs through the home to the narrow door in the city wall. The guards there are frozen, waiting with drawn weapons. "Open the door," he yells at them.

"What?" one of the boys replies, incredulous.

Joshua hastily explains, "Unbar the door. That is their mother out there."

When the young man stands there looking perplexed, Joshua shoves him away and opens the door. Gomer almost falls in, exhausted from her journey and ecstatic for her hard-won sanctuary, however temporary that may be.

"Thank God," Joshua exclaims.

She looks at him, then at the guards. "My children?"

They run to her from around the corner, and stumbling to them in tears, she grabs them close, clutching them to her body.

Joshua then addresses the gawking would-be soldiers. "Well, bar the door," he directs.

Then Gomer and her children move to the other room, as their friend follows. "Thank you for staying with them," Gomer expresses.

Joshua brings her some water. After gulping it down, she then looks around as if something is missing. What is it, she thinks. Then she realizes. Hosea. To her astonishment, she's missing Hosea. "Where is He? Where is my husband?"

Joshua answers, "He was here, he went to the palace not long ago."

"He said he would return," Not-loved declares.

Gomer shakes her head in distress. "He is wasting his time at the palace," she explains. "The army is taking the city today. The entire hill is surrounded, and they have already broken through the main gate."

"We need to tell Father," Not-loved cries, now concerned for him.

Gomer holds her children, wondering about her path and weighing her choice. Why does she want to find her husband, what strange fate pushes her desire toward him after all these years? And caressing Not-mine atop the head, she thinks, how can she leave her children after fighting up the Watchtower Hill to be reunited with them?

As Not-mine buries his face in the folds of Gomer's clothes, Not-loved watches her mother's face, as if she reads her mind.

"I will go find Hosea," Joshua announces.

His statement, at first, puts Gomer's mind at ease. Yes, her place is with her children. She reasons, Joshua will go, Hosea's long-time friend, and if it can be done, he will bring Hosea back here, for them all to be together one last time. Yet something in her heart tells her this is not meant to be, that there is a different destiny she is meant to embrace at the end.

Screams of war break her thoughts and looking out the home she notices how the day has grown dark. Is it so late? Has evening come or does the smoke of battle blot out the sun, she wonders.

Joshua and the band of boys look out at the streets, at the burning homes and the Assyrian soldiers already within their city. They close the door and proclaim, "They are coming."

"What do we do?" one of the boy soldiers asks.

The youngest and, thus far, quietest of the guards is still in the room within the wall by the barred door, staring around the interior. "Is this room inside the city wall?" he asks.

Joshua believes this must be the first time he has spoken at all.

"The barracks has places like this," he continues. "But everywhere else is just rubble filling in the casemate construction." He looks at the smaller brick façade walls closing in the room between the greater walls of stone blocks. "These bricks should be thin here. If we can break through them, we can get to the rubble inside."

"And?" asks Joshua.

"We can pile the rubble inside the home, masking this room, and you and the family hide within. In the chaos hopefully the Assyrians will think this home has already been destroyed and abandoned."

Everyone looks at the boy, but Gomer looks even harder at the young man. "He-helps? Is that you?"

Suddenly quiet again, he simply nods in affirmation.

Then Joshua too looks at him, now with recognition. "Why did you not say something before?"

He-helps shrugs.

"This just might work," Joshua agrees.

They all grab what they can to break through the bricks, and begin piling the rubble from the city wall, covering up the inner room. The guards in training help on the other side, within the home. Then, when satisfied with their work they run out to join the fight against the enemy.

As Joshua listens to the battle outside, Gomer quietly coos over her children.

Ω

Alone in the palace, Hosea makes his way into the audience chamber where the King's throne is veiled. The great room is white, silent, and empty. "Is there anyone here?" his voice echoes back to himself.

He begins to walk toward the dais when from behind the curtain, the voice of the King answers, "I am. And you are."

With sudden force, the veil is ripped down by the King and he lets it fall, fluttering from the stage. He is made up as before, as a quiet glory remains, but otherwise his presence is newly downcast. "I will not be needing that anymore."

The King now turns his attention to the Prophet, his royal person walking down from his high place. Face to face, these two men who share a name of salvation, one political and another religious, now find that salvation for the city escapes them both. "I suppose out of all my subjects, it would be the most boring of them to treat with me at the last."

Hosea ignores the slight. In a hurry, he exclaims, "The Assyrians are here at your doorstep. What do you plan to do? Your people wait for your word."

The King, seeming more bothered by Hosea's presence than that of the invading army, gives him an inquisitive look. "Why do you seem so surprised? The one who has been speaking of this very event my entire reign. You know as well as I do what is at the door." His royal mask seems to fade, revealing an undone person, as he explains, "I have tried to keep it at bay, but now there is nothing left to do. It may wear the guise of the Assyrians, but it is death that comes for us. We will all die, choose now how best to do so."

Hosea gestures around. "Where are your guard and officers?"

"Out there, being gallant. Fight if you want and be cut down, my own guard has been dismissed to do so. Flee and be ridden down. Accept the inevitable with grace, beg for your life, or make amends with what little time is left," the King states. Then pointing to the stage of his rule, he says, "I will wait for it here, as the dead monarch that I am."

They are interrupted by shouts and screams, heard along with a low rumble and a deafening shatter. "Do you hear? They are coming," the King warns Hosea. "Go to your family, it is all that is left to you, and even that is brief."

Hosea hears and looks for an exit. He has wasted his time here, he thinks. And now he is left to die with this madman. "How? There is no escape."

"You will find momentary salvation in our Covenant. The rest is up to you."

Hosea searches as the sound of armed death marches nearer. Then he sees the ivory replica of the Ark of the Covenant. Running toward it, he finds that the lid opens onto an abyss just large enough to squeeze through. The King walks back up to await his fate upon his throne, and Hosea escapes as the invaders break into the chamber.

Ω

Inside the small walled-in room, Gomer's children and Joshua wait with her in the dark and quiet, as the sounds of battle disperse. Then a commotion of sliding rocks is heard above them, and a hand is seen between the rubble within the wall and the top of the wood slat roof.

The hand waves at them and then disappears, as a voice whispers down to them, "It's me, He-helps." His slender body slides into view feet first and then he addresses them. "The main force of Assyrians has moved through the city. Now only individual soldiers bent on chaos wander the burning streets looking for survivors."

"What about the others with you?" asks Joshua.

He-helps bends his head down in shame. "They all fell. I ran and hid. After the battle, I was able to move about, but very carefully. I climbed up here to the top of the wall."

"Were you seen?" Gomer asks.

"No. The day is unnaturally dark, and smoke conceals everything."

"Good," Gomer thinks aloud.

They all look at her.

"I am going to find Hosea."

The two men disagree with her, believing she should stay with the children.

But Not-loved looks at her mother and knows what must be done. "Go," she says.

Joshua still tries to persuade her against this action. "One of us should go instead or at least accompany you. What if he is already dead?" he says.

"No. He is alive, our fate is bound together," Gomer assures. "And you should stay here. For so long you have been a friend to this family. We need you now as ever, the children need you. They are yours as much as Hosea's and mine. And He-helps is the only one with a sword."

She kisses her children one last time then gives the dagger of the fallen-star goddess to her daughter. "Keep this on you. She will protect you." Then she leaves the same way He-helps came down.

Left to her own inner power, Not-loved is at peace as if she has read the cosmic signs of her parents and knows that the time for their alignment has come. She comforts her little brother, as well as the two men.

Ω

A false panel of relief artwork on the palace wall, depicting the powerful cherubim with flaming sword guarding the gate of Eden, opens and Hosea steps out into the desolation. His face reflects the carnage.

What is this, he inquires without words.

Walking among the corpses strewn about the court before the broken palace doors, Hosea is stricken by the sight. His mind clamoring out to his God, he thinks, is this the justice I have prophesied? This is wanton slaughter.

Then he sees the worst. He sees the young boy who was sorry for having played a game with a stick and a girl, now dead, struck by many wounds.

And Hosea breaks.

Some new apocalypse tears through all his previous revelations, all the things that built him up as the voice of a jealous God, and now lays him bare, all razed down to his human foundations. "What is this? Lord, what is this?" he howls. "Is this what I have served? This is unjust. Undeserved. Such reckless hate for a benign inequity of loving the feminine." He beats his chest and tears his clothes. "These people deserved love, not to be thrown to Gehenna. What have I done? What great sin have I sown?"

He holds the boy's corpse and pleads with him through sobbing, "Forgive me. Is it too late? Forgive me." Without an answer, Hosea gives his own. "It is too late. I am damned," he wails.

A great shadow gathers around him. "Even now, the darkness swallows me up. Where is the light?" He looks up to find the sun high in the sky, yet a black abyss growing at the edge, and he quickly looks away. "What is this new revelation?" Is there yet time, even now at the end, for true salvation, he wonders. He must find her. His deliverance has always been with her, his beloved. He has been blind in the light, but now, in this darkness, he sees.

Ω

The air is thick with black resinous smoke, as Gomer walks through the city. She witnesses the unrestrained death and destruction, bodies of men, women, and children crumpled onto the streets. And as her eyes move over the horror, they weep without her knowing.

Then the world begins to darken strangely, even as a wind blows at the tattered towers of smoke. And she gazes upward to a clear sky far above and unconcerned with their devastation, seeing the sun itself begin to shut its rays from them. Somehow this omen renews her purpose as she realizes she must be near the palace courtyard. However, she is stopped by screams coming from a nearby home.

Hesitating only a moment, she rushes through the door of the house. There, a giant of a soldier is over a young woman beating helplessly against him. Without thinking, reacting on instinct for the sake of all the dead and violated, Gomer takes a spear from a fallen guard and shrieks as she runs the blade toward the monster's back.

But the shaft breaks upon impact on his armor and the soldier turns from his victim to Gomer, who now stands in his shadow. She begins to back away as he advances but his reach is too long, and he grabs her with both hands by the neck, lifting her into the air as his grip tightens around her throat.

Her eyes begin to grow dark. But then the giant makes a queer gargling sound and drops Gomer to the floor. And a sword slides through and out the front of his groin. The ogre falls to his knees as the young woman wrenches his own weapon back out of him and hacks his head off in four cumbersome swings from the large iron blade. Dropping the sword with a clangor, she runs past Gomer, out into the streets. And Gomer sits up, catching her breath.

Ω

Hosea now stands amidst the slaughter with new determination and makes his way through the courtyard of Sheol, when a young woman painted with blood runs from an open door and past him down the street. He moves away from the place and toward the southern wall of the city as fire begins to rise from the Ivory Palace.

Staying close to the buildings and out of sight from the open streets he makes his way back to his family home and finds the door thrown down and the front timbers set aflame. He runs in and discovers the rubble over the outer door. Fearing the worst, he begins to dig his way through, bruising and bloodying his hands. He cries out for Gomer and his children, then stops at the sound of a small voice behind the wreckage. "Father?"

Beginning again in earnest, he is met in the middle as those in the hidden room dig to him. Covered in dust, he and his children embrace. Then looking around for his beloved, he asks, "Where is She? Where is my wife?"

"She went to find you. Mother loves you, Father," Not-loved exclaims.

"And I love her." Then Hosea declares to them, "Come, you're getting out of here."

"But where is there to go?" Joshua asks. "The enemy moves here and there in the streets and the whole city is ringed in from the outside."

"I know a way," he says, looking at his old family door in the wall. He unbars it and cracks it open. And looking out, Hosea speaks to his friend, "The way is clear. Go to my family's old storage building where we used to play as children. Do you remember my hiding place in the floor?"

Joshua nods in affirmation.

"It tunnels all the way down the hill and beyond into the wilderness. Take the children and go."

"What about you?"

Hosea smiles for them all.

"Father is going to Mother," his daughter says with glee.

"I Am. I have forgotten myself, and I am not whole without her." He kisses his children. "You are Mine. And you are Loved." Then laying his hand on Joshua's shoulder, he tells him, "Take them, my friend. Now."

Hosea leaves once more into the City of Shomron, as Joshua and the children dash out into the open, running toward the old shed, and accompanied by He-helps with his rusty sword.

But then as they throw open the door, they despair at the sight of a great haystack piled high above their way of escape.

"Not-loved?" Joshua begins speaking.

"It is Loved now," she plainly states. "And my brother is Mine."

"Yes, you are right," Joshua says. He looks at the children with care. "You have always been Loved and Mine."

Then he tells her, "Please, see to your brother." And Joshua turns his attention to He-helps. "Help me with the hay."

Ω

Through the smoke and under the darkened sun, Hosea seeks for Gomer.

"My beloved?"

Ω

Surrounded by flames and unnatural shadow, Gomer searches for Hosea.

"Where are you?"

Ω

Loved looks out while Joshua and He-helps pitch tufts of hay with their long forks out from over the hidden passage. "It is getting darker. The sun is being blot out by a great shadow and the smoke rises to meet it," she says.

"We are almost done," Joshua replies, breathing through his hurried work.

Loved strains to see further out and spies shadows moving, coming closer to them. "Soldiers," she cries.

"Where?"

"Coming this way. I think they know we are here."

He-helps trades the pitchfork for his sword and recklessly runs out and toward the advancing shades.

"Wait," Joshua calls out.

He only goes a few paces from the door before falling from two arrows in his chest.

"They are coming now, fast," Loved warns.

Joshua shoves the last mound of hay aside, uncovering their hope. "I have it. Go, go now."

Loved grabs Mine and slides into the tunnel, then looks back for her friend.

"I said go. Do not look back," Joshua tells her.

Loved and Mine disappear into the black and Joshua frantically searches the shed. What he finds, among the mess of straw, are multiple cases of oil and a tinder box.

As the first soldier runs in, Joshua, the truest friend to Hosea and his family, engulfs them both with flames, burning along with the shed, and ensuring that Loved and Mine's way of escape is not discovered.

Ω

As the sun and moon near total eclipse, He begins to despair. Graciously, a wind blows, swirling away the smoke and fanning the flames to brighten the way before him. He finds himself at the market where He used to watch his beloved from afar. And there, once more across from him, She stands amidst the ash of the burning city. They are both frozen in place at the sudden appearance of their mutual desire.

"The children?" She asks.

Ω

Loved and Mine are born again, unseen, from a small opening of rock into the wilderness, far past the war ringed hill. The children, male and female, stand hand in hand, then begin to walk south through the trees. Without looking back, they leave Shomron and its burning city crown and the black abysmal sun hovering over all.

Ω

He and She run to each other, collapsing into one another's arms.

"You were right."

"No. I was wrong, I am sorry."

The moon covers the sun and transforms it into a black hole hanging over the great hill, a celestial void birthing something new into the destruction of the old.

And there amidst the flames, She and He know each other.

In the Fullness of Time

"Yeshua said to them, When you make the two into one, and when you make the inner like the outer…and the upper like the lower, and when you make male and female into a single one, so that the male will not be male nor the female be female…then you will enter the kingdom."

– The Gospel of Thomas

Witness their completion!

The City on a Hill burns, an alchemical vessel of death and birth, the threshold doors broken and cast down.

As the void above first moves, giving back a ray of light, from out that torn gate come They, the Divine Androgyne, cartwheeling down the Watchtower Hill and laughing with themself in love and bliss.

And the world cannot hold them back, and so is transformed along with them.

THANK YOU TO MY PATRONS

Jordan Desmarais, David Dickerson, Kalen Flansburg, Morgan Ashton Griffin, James "Bucky" Jackson, courtney marie, Ethan Parker McClure, Meagan Metcalf, Richard Novak, Phil and Monica Robertson, and Preston and Kim Wyatt

And a special thanks to Kenzie. This book would not exist without you.

ABOUT THE AUTHOR

Clent Roye Wyatt is an author, poet, performance artist, and stay-at-home dad living in North Texas. He has had poetry featured in *What Now?* an art and news magazine published locally in Denton by Spiderweb Salon, *Pens and Lenses*, a 2021 poetry and photography show at The Greater Denton Arts Council, and as a part of the *collective/connection* interactive poetry installation at the Dallas Museum of Art's C3 Gallery. He was also chosen as a finalist for *The Banyan Review*'s 2023 Poetry Prize.

Finding himself in a time and place where all things, even people, are commodified and branded, Clent seeks to infuse his work with a sense of the sacred and the mythic.